Wright's father ran a station on the
...erground Railroad, the route by which
...roes were helped to escape from slav-
... in the South to freedom in Canada.
...s was a dangerous undertaking in 1851,
...n slave-trackers and Federal Marshals
...e trying to track down fugitives and
...roy the Underground.

...ess had been brought up to believe that
...ryone had the right to liberty, and this
...ef was strengthened by contact with
... Negroes his father helped. When his
...r brother was sent to prison, Jess at
...rteen was at last given a chance for
...on. He and his friend Sven, pursued by
...ederal Marshal, had to help two escap-
...; slaves reach the next station on their
...ficult road to freedom.

...n the nineteenth century, hundreds of
...milies in the North risked much to carry
... the dangerous work of the Underground
...ilroad. Bianca Bradbury, author of
...any successful historical novels, has
...rned her talent to the story of a boy and
...s family who played a part in that work.

...he Author: Three of Mrs. Bradbury's last
...x books have been Junior Literary Guild
...lections. She and her husband live in
...ew Milford, Connecticut, and she is the
...other of two grown sons.

THE UNDERGROUNDERS

Books for Older Girls

BY BIANCA BRADBURY

Amethyst Summer

Goodness and Mercy Jenkins

Shoes in September

Laughter in Our House

Flight Into Spring

Laurie

THE
UNDERGROUNDERS

by Bianca Bradbury

Illustrated by Jon Nielsen

IVES WASHBURN, Inc. : NEW YORK

IVES WASHBURN, INC. Publishers

750 Third Avenue, New York, N.Y. 10017

THE UNDERGROUNDERS

LIBRARY OF CONGRESS CATALOG CARD NUMBER: 66-14236

MANUFACTURED IN THE UNITED STATES OF AMERICA

THE UNDERGROUNDERS

CHAPTER ONE

THE DAY was clear and bright, but Jess pulled the buffalo robe up higher. This November of 1851 was turning out to be a cold, windy month. Jess glanced at his father, hoping he would speak. He also wished his father would give Major a slap of the reins and hurry him on home, but Major was old and liked to take his own time.

Mr. Wright seemed lost in thought. Finally, Jess couldn't stand it any longer. "Father, why were you so anxious to see Sheriff Hodgkins?" he asked. "Was it about the Negroes you hid in the barn last night?"

That caught his father's attention, all right. He swiveled around on the buggy seat. "You knew they were there, Jess?"

"Yes, I knew they were there."

Mr. Wright hesitated. Jess waited. Finally, his father said reluctantly, "Son, I suppose the time has come when you'll have to know what's going on." Then he stopped, shielding his eyes against the late afternoon sun. "Look, there's a wagon, and it's coming fast."

Jess stood up in the buggy. "It's ours. Pa, Ben's using his whip on Leftfoot. Something's wrong!"

"Whoa!" Mr. Wright shouted. Major stopped so short, Jess almost pitched over the front rail.

The wagon kept coming. Jess's brother was standing,

1

cracking the whip over Leftfoot's back, the wagon bouncing, slewing from side to side. Mr. Wright leaped down to the road. The wagon came abreast. Ben didn't slacken speed, but yelled, "Pa, don't stop me! Get along home!" He passed his father, standing there in the road.

Grim-faced, Mr. Wright climbed back in, jerked the reins, and swung Major around in the narrow, dirt road. By the time the buggy was headed back to town, the wagon was out of sight beyond a hill. "Father, what's wrong?" Jess asked. He hung on tight, and his heart was pounding so hard it ached in his breast.

Major whinnied indignantly but obeyed the whip snapping about his ears. The buggy reached the top of the hill. A hundred yards further on, the wagon was standing in the middle of the highway. A stranger was leaning out of his saddle, holding Leftfoot's reins. A second man, red-faced and angry, was trying to control his own dancing horse.

Mr. Wright brought Major to a stop. Jess saw that his face was ashen. He slowly climbed down, and it seemed to Jess he moved like an old, old man. Jess jumped out of his side of the buggy, and his father saw that and ordered, "Get back in. No matter what happens, stay in the buggy."

It didn't occur to Jess to disobey, for Mr. Wright's word was law to both his sons. He watched his father approach the group, but he was too far away to hear. They talked for a moment. Then the riders went to the back of the wagon and pulled away some light hay, tossing it out in the road. One shouted, "Come out of there!" and snatched away a piece of carpet.

Two men slowly crawled out of the wagon, and Jess saw that they were dressed in rags and that they were

2

black. One, the older, seemed to be crying, and the other started to run. Ben leaped from the wagon and caught him, and Jess wondered why, but then saw the reason. The strange man held a pistol leveled at the Negro's back.

Jess couldn't help it; he was crying too, with fear.

Waving the pistol, the man gestured for the Negroes to get back into the wagon. His partner was doing something to Ben. He helped Ben into the wagon too, and then Jess realized why his brother submitted so meekly. Ben's hands were tied behind his back.

The horsemen remounted and waited, watching while Mr. Wright walked back to where Jess sat. "There's trouble," he said. "I have to drive the wagon. Take Major back to the farm and stay there. Tell your mother I'll be home as quick as I can and that she's not to worry——"

Jess broke in, "Who are those men? What are they doing to Ben?"

Mr. Wright shook his head. Jess had to sit there helplessly and watch while his father returned to the wagon, climbed up to the high seat, and picked up Leftfoot's reins. The unknown horsemen rode like guards, one on each side. The cavalcade disappeared around the next bend, on the road to town.

Three hours later, Jess Wright was waiting in the barn for his father to come. Early dusk had settled down. His mother waited too, in the lamplit kitchen, and Jess knew she was crying.

Jess was only fourteen, but he was tall and stocky for his age. He felt like a man, and he intended to have a show-down with his father. It was high time he did.

For two months, secret things had been happening at the Wright farm. His parents and Ben had never discussed them with Jess, but he wasn't stupid. He knew that his father and his brother had been helping Negroes escape from slavery in the South up to freedom in Canada. It was a dangerous business, and Jess felt he was old enough to be included in it.

Shivering in his denim shirt, he hitched his pants up and sat on a barrel to wait. He was thinking of wrapping himself in a horse blanket when he heard Leftfoot and the wagon clattering up the lane.

He caught the reins, while his father climbed down. "Thank you, son," Mr. Wright said. "Take care of Leftfoot, will you?"

He turned toward the house. Jess knew he wanted to find his wife, to comfort her. "Father, I have to talk to you," he said in a low voice.

Mr. Wright hesitated. "Can it wait until I see your mother and tell her about Ben?"

"Yes, sir."

"I'll come back as soon as I've spoken with her."

Jess busied himself wiping Leftfoot down. His father still didn't come, so he combed out the horse's thick black mane and tail. Leftfoot snorted and complained. Like many old horses, his chief interest was his next meal, and he kept jerking his head, turning his eyes reproachfully on his young master. Jess finally led him into the box stall and pulled down hay. He was setting out to draw a pail of water from the well when his father crossed the barnyard.

An old carriage seat leaned against the barn, and Mr. Wright said tiredly, "Let's sit down. You want to hear about Ben."

"Yes, Pa. I feel I've got a right."

His father glanced up, surprised, but agreed, "Yes, you have a right. You and your brother are very close, and that's a good thing. Ben's in jail."

6

"What happened to those two Negroes you hid in the barn last night?"

"One of the men you saw was a slave catcher from Maryland. He had tracked them up here to Jericho. The other man was a United States marshal. They made our Sheriff Hodgkins tell where the runaways were probably hidden. Hodgkins sent somebody to warn us, but Ben didn't get away in time. The last I saw of those two poor souls they were chained together in that scoundrel slave catcher's buggy, setting out for Maryland."

Jess said angrily, "I thought Sheriff Hodgkins was a good man. He must have guessed that you and Ben were running a station in the underground railroad, but he didn't interfere before."

"Maybe he wanted to look the other way and make believe he didn't know," Mr. Wright said. "He's like a lot of people here in the North. He hasn't made up his mind how he really feels about slavery. He isn't a bad man. But now this new law, this Fugitive Slave Law, has changed everything. It punishes any local sheriff who refuses to help a federal marshal catch a runaway slave. It also sets a six months' sentence in jail and a thousand dollars fine for people like us who help them escape. That government marshal wanted to see me put in jail too, but the sheriff refused."

Jess started to speak, but his father added, "Don't tell your mother how heavy Ben's sentence might be. She's worried enough. Let's see what the court does in Ben's case."

The kitchen door opened, and Lavinia Wright's sweet voice called, "Boys, supper's ready."

"Come on," Mr. Wright said.

Jess stopped him. "Pa, I want to take Ben's place."

7

"What do you mean, Jess?"

"I'm old enough and big enough."

"What makes you think I'm going on with the work, in face of this new law, in face of what's happened to Ben?"

"Aren't you?" Jess asked.

"Boys, where are you?" Mrs. Wright called. "Supper's getting cold."

"After we eat we'll talk about this," Jess's father promised.

Mrs. Wright's face was serene, but her eyes were dark-circled and looked haunted. She dished up the food while the men washed at the sink. The table, with its turkey-red cloth, looked nice as it always did, but she had made one mistake; she had set Ben's place as usual. When they sat down, Ben's empty chair faced them.

They bent their heads, and Mr. Wright said grace. Jess just caught his mother's whisper, "Dear God, take care of my son."

His father served the fried steak and turnip. "Is somebody taking food to Ben?" Mrs. Wright asked.

"Yes, Viney," her husband said gently. "Mrs. Hodgkins feeds the prisoners in the town jail, and they say she's a real good cook."

"Just the same, I'm going to take him a basket tomorrow." Mrs. Wright's voice broke, but she went on, "I never expected I'd ever set foot inside the jail to see one of my menfolk, but tomorrow I'll go to see my son. A few folks in this town approve of what we're doing, but a good many will think we're just common criminals. If they all see me going into the jail I won't care. I won't be ashamed."

"No, Viney, you won't be ashamed," Mr. Wright said softly. Jess glanced away, for the way his parents looked at each other across the table was too intimate and sacred for a third person to see. Their eyes met and held, with love and respect.

"I'm going too," Jess said gruffly.

That broke the spell that held his parents. "Of course you can see your brother," Mr. Wright said.

He struck the table then with the flat of his hand, and started up out of his chair. "For the first time in my life I forgot about the milking!"

"Jess did it before you came home," his wife told him.

"Imagine forgetting a thing like that! How's Opal?"

"I think she'll have her calf before morning," Jess told him.

"We'll check on her before we go to bed."

A sickle moon lit the barnyard as they crossed it, Jess carrying the lantern. Opal was restless when they looked at her, and Jess forked down hay to give her comfortable bedding, while his father stroked her neck.

They were standing in the wide door, looking up at the sky-full of brilliant stars, when a horse cantered up the lane. Jess started to douse the lantern, but his father said, "There's no need to do that. We're not hiding anyone to-night."

The rider trotted up and dismounted, and they saw his long, red beard and recognized Eben Fuller, who was an undergrounder, too. He kept a station for hiding slaves in Smithtown, a village ten miles south of Jericho. "Evening, Joe," he said, then hesitated.

"It's all right to talk in front of Jess," Mr. Wright said.

"I hear they caught your older boy and the two folks I brought to you last night."

"That's so. The federal marshal took them away. Ben's in jail."

"Well?" Mr. Fuller asked.

9

"Well, what?"

"Are you through with this business, Joe? Do you want to drop out of the underground? If you do, I don't blame you. It's asking too much to expect you to go on. Your wife ought to have a say in the matter, too. Now we know they plan to enforce that vicious law they passed in Washington last year. How can you run this farm without Ben if he gets a stiff sentence? Some of the others in the movement asked me to tell you that they want to help you pay the fine. I won't mention any names; it's best that way. We feel that the burden's too heavy on you now, and we ought to try to find somebody else to run this Jericho station, to hide the fugitives and pass them north."

After he finished there was a silence. Mr. Wright broke it. "I know what we're going to do."

"What have you decided?"

"We'll go on. This infamous new law puts an even greater burden on us, to help the Negroes on their way to freedom."

"How does your wife feel about it?"

"We haven't discussed it, but I know she's not ashamed of what happened to Ben," Mr. Wright said.

"I didn't think she would be. She's a fine woman. Going to jail in a good cause will be something your Ben will be proud of for the rest of his life. I'm glad you're staying in the work. It would be mighty hard to set up a new station in this northwest corner of Connecticut. Don't let your independence stop you from letting us help pay Ben's fine, though. We've got a right to help. It was only bad luck that he was caught, not one of the others in the underground."

"Have you any idea when more fugitives will be com-

10

ing?" Mr. Wright asked. "I've got a good hiding place for them under the barn, but now that winter's coming I want to fix a place in the house."

"I can't say," Mr. Fuller told him. "I never know until they knock at my door."

Jess held the horse while the visitor mounted. Mr. Fuller called, "Good night," and rode away.

Mrs. Wright was sewing in the parlor when they came in. The round stove made an island of warmth against the cold of the night. She looked up. "I heard a rider. Was it Eben Fuller?"

"Yes, Lavinia."

"He wants you to go on with the work."

"Yes, Lavinia."

"If I said, 'No, I can't bear any more; it's put one of my sons behind prison bars, and that's enough,' what would you say then, Joe?"

"I'd listen, and weigh your opinions," her husband said. "I ought to tell you that Eben offered to let me out of my promise to help."

His wife said slowly, "I've thought it over and decided not to ask you to give it up. Ben's getting caught doesn't change the fact that those poor souls need our help."

Her husband bent and kissed her. "Thank you, Viney. But now I'll have to tell you the rest of it. Jess wants to take Ben's place."

"No! He's only a schoolboy!"

Jess knew better than to plead and beg. The habit of obeying his elders without argument was too strong. His parents would decide, and nothing he said would change their decision.

His father stated Jess's case for him. "He's big for his

11

age," Mr. Wright pointed out. "He's strong, and he's fair to middling bright, and he wants to help."

Jess's mother said sharply, "I say again, No! This is no game for a boy to play, to brag about to his friends."

Jess's temper flared up then. "Mother, I know it's no game, and I would never breathe a word to anybody!"

Her face softened. "I apologize, son. I know you wouldn't. I'm upset tonight, and that's my only excuse for saying such a belittling thing. But this affair is men's business, for it means breaking the law, and it's very dangerous. Tell me honestly, Jess, why you think your father and I should allow you. Forget that it might be exciting. Give me a better reason than just the fact that you want to."

Jess had the sinking feeling he was arguing a lost cause, but he tried to think of the best reason he could offer. His mother was no helpless, weak woman, but a strong force in the family, and her word was almost as powerful as her husband's. Jess sweated, knowing that what he said could make all the difference.

He remembered what a preacher had said, a few weeks earlier, when he stopped in and stayed for a meal. The Reverend Sykes belonged to the underground too, and was famous in the movement for his nerve and skill in hiding and transporting the runaway slaves. He had quoted from the Bible, "Let the oppressed go free. Betray not him who wandereth."

Jess said steadily, "I feel as you and Pa do. It's as the Reverend Sykes said that time he came here. It's a matter of plain right and wrong. I don't believe any man has the right to hold a man or woman or child in bondage, whether they're black or white. If you'll let me work with Pa, I'll be careful and obey him in all ways. And I'll never

12

talk but will keep mum. Besides, Pa will need me. He can't run the farm and carry on this work too."

His mother's look was straight and direct. "This ugly thing, slavery, weighs on you as it does on us, Jess?"

"Yes, ma'am." Jess was beginning to feel hopeful.

His mother said slowly, "You can help, son, but not in the way you wish. A heavy share of the running of the farm will come down on you, with Ben away. If you do that you'll be doing your part. But I cannot, in good conscience, give permission to let you do any transporting of slaves. You're just too young."

That was that. Mr. Wright said, "I agree, Viney. You're right, as always. And there's plenty Jess can do to help without running the risks."

"You'd both better get busy right away fixing a refuge inside the house," Mrs. Wright told them. "I didn't sleep a wink last night thinking of those two hiding in that cold hole under the barn. Poor souls," she murmured, "poor, poor souls. I wonder where they are now. What will happen once their master gets them back to Maryland? He might beat them to death for the trouble they caused him. Will they ever get free again?"

"We've got to put that part out of our minds," her husband said heavily. "We cannot take on the whole burden of every slave in the South. We can only do our part and help them when we get the chance. Let's go to bed now. Morning will come soon enough."

Long after his parents were asleep, Jess stared through his window, watching the moon sliding down the sky. The hot soapstone his mother had wrapped in flannel to warm his feet gradually grew cold, but the feather quilt made his bed wonderfully comfortable.

Jess thought of Ben, whom he loved. Had the sheriff's wife given his brother a good thick blanket for his iron bed in the jail?

He would see his brother tomorrow. Ben would ask how their father was going to carry on the underground work alone. Oh, how Jess wished he could tell him that he, Jess, was taking Ben's place!

CHAPTER TWO

DAWN CAME all too soon. Jess found his clothes in the gray light and still half asleep stumbled downstairs. His mother was putting up his lunch for school. A lantern in the barn showed that his father had started the milking. Jess pulled on his heavy wool coat and crossed the barnyard. Puddles were covered by a skim of ice.

Opal had delivered her calf, and it leaned against her, a beautiful little brown and white creature, bawling loudly. Steam rose from the other cows, fastened to their stanchions along the center of the barn, and Mr. Wright was halfway along the line. He looked up from the cow he was milking to say, "Morning, Jess. First take care of Opal."

The rest of the herd would be turned out after they were milked, but Opal would be kept in for a few days. Jess filled her pail of water at the pump in the yard, and set it inside the stall, and let down hay for her, and filled the bin with chopped corn.

Morning chores took a full two hours. After he let out the cows, to find what winter grass there was in the home lot, Jess carried the milk to the house. He fed the work horses, Star and Leftfoot, and turned them out. Then he helped his father shovel the manure into a wheelbarrow and dumped it on the pile behind the barn. The Wrights took satisfaction in keeping their place clean and neat.

Mrs. Wright served their breakfast. As soon as he had

15

eaten, Jess filled the woodboxes in the kitchen and parlor and carried out yesterday's ashes. Then he took his books and lunch pail and set out for the Pumpkin Hollow school, two miles away.

As usual, his friend Sven Swanson was waiting in the road at the end of the Swansons' lane. They walked in silence. Sven seemed to be struggling to say something. What it was Jess didn't know, for Sven didn't succeed in getting it out.

Other boys waiting in the schoolyard weren't so shy. Jess had a lot of friends in that school, but he had one real enemy, Sim Slaney. Sim was sixteen years old, six feet tall, and a born trouble-maker. He lived on the mountain. He had a sour smell about him, and his ragged hair hung to his shoulders.

His reason for hating Jess was solid enough. Jess's father had recently caught Sim's father red-handed in the act of stealing harness from the Wrights' barn, and had seen to it the thief was punished.

Now Sim pushed through the small children waiting for the door to open. He planted himself in front of Jess and Sven, blocking their path, and tossed back his greasy black hair. "We had a bet on," he said. "We bet you wouldn't show your face this morning. How does it feel to have a jailbird in your family, Jess?"

"Look who's talking about having a jailbird in his family," Sven began.

"Leave him to me," Jess warned his friend. He wasn't afraid. He and Sim had squared off before, and he knew Sim would give way if he showed fight. Sim's friends were circling around too, but Jess still wasn't afraid. This gang who lived up on the mountain might think they were wild and lawless, but they knuckled under if they were opposed. Ben had taught Jess how to fight and win, and Jess in turn had taught the other boys in the Pumpkin Hollow school, so they could keep the mountain gang in line.

The schoolmaster, Mr. House, appeared at the door then, clanging the bell. He saw that a fight was brewing and strode across the yard, collared Sim, and pushed him into the schoolhouse.

Long ago, the town fathers of Jericho had given up hiring a woman for school marm. A girl could handle the small children, but only a strong man could keep order and beat some knowledge into the heads of grown farm boys. Mr. House wasn't afraid of using the ruler or the strap.

Jess, like the others, pretended he hated Mr. House, because he too had felt the full weight of that three foot, brass-bound ruler. Secretly, he liked and admired him. Mr. House stood up to the bullies even when they ganged up on him, and, furthermore, he cared about education. School was open only during the winter months when the children weren't needed on the farms. Mr. House took pride in pounding as much learning as he could into their heads, during those four months.

The small boys and girls had the front desks. The older ones sat in back, the girls taking the choice seats near the stove. Sim sat directly behind Jess.

Mr. House banged on his desk for order. Sim must have been feeling really brave that morning, for he paid no attention. "Phew!" he exclaimed, "Phew! I smell jail!"

The room was absolutely silent. There wasn't a sound. Jess went icy cold, for now he realized that everybody knew about Ben.

Mr. House said quietly, "Sim, say exactly what you mean."

"I mean that Jess Wright stinks of jail, and why wouldn't he? That's where his brother is."

"Do you know why Ben Wright is in jail?"

"Sure. Everybody knows. For helping the darkies."

Mr. House said, "The correct word is 'Negroes.' We'll discuss this matter later during history lesson."

The hours went all too fast for Jess. Although his seat was a long way from the stove, his hands were wet with perspiration. Every time he looked up from his book, the eyes of his schoolmates were on him. What was Mr. House going to say? It was terribly important to Jess to learn how the schoolmaster felt about this problem.

The last period, the history hour came. Mr. House didn't open the book but stepped forward. He began, "What we're going to talk about is living history, not dry historical facts in a book, and you children are a part of it. You know that this country is torn by this problem of slavery. Up here in the North it hasn't seemed very close to us. Now, it is becoming our problem, too. In increasing numbers the slaves are escaping from their masters, trying to get north to Canada, to freedom. It's no secret that they follow regular routes. One of the most important runs through this western part of Connecticut, comes right through our own town. The runaways come over from the west, from New York state, or up from the shore when they've made their escape by ship from southern ports.

"People don't talk about this very much. We've guessed that some of our fellow townsmen were helping the fugitives.

"I'm not going to tell you what is right and what is wrong. You children, like your parents, will have to decide that for yourselves. In the United States we believe in rule by law. Those who are helping the slaves feel that the

Fugitive Slave Law is unjust, and they have good reasons for feeling that way. Those on the other side believe that the law must be obeyed, that if it's a bad law it must be changed but not broken.

"Now let's speak about Jess's brother. We all know and like Ben Wright. We're sorry he's in jail. I want you older children to understand this and understand it well. We mustn't condemn Ben because he broke the law in what he believes is a good cause. At the same time, we mustn't excuse lawlessness. If each man decided for himself what laws he chose to obey and what he chose to disobey, we would have anarchy in the United States and no real government. That is all I have to say. School is dismissed."

What Mr. House said cleared the air. On the way home Sven talked freely. He seemed to think that Ben was a hero. Jess answered his friend's questions carefully, giving him no real information. But Jess's heart felt lighter. All the children had looked at him with new eyes after the schoolmaster made his little speech. At least they knew now why the Wright family didn't feel disgraced and wasn't ashamed because one of its members was in jail.

His father had the buggy ready when he reached home. A basket of food was stowed under the seat. The three drove to town.

Townspeople stared openly as Major trotted along Main Street. Mrs. Wright kept her head high, looking neither to left nor right. Her husband drove around in back of the town hall, leaving the horse and buggy in the carriage shed. "Bring the basket, Jess," he ordered. "Come, Lavinia."

The jail was in the cellar of the town hall. They started down the outside stairs and an awful smell met them, of dirt and stale sweat and dampness. Mrs. Wright swayed,

19

and Jess thought she was going to faint. Then she got hold of herself.

Constable Johnson was sitting at a desk. Ben was lying on an iron cot in one cell and the other cell was empty.

Mr. Johnson shambled to his feet. "Good day, Mrs. Wright," he stammered.

If he expected her to act shy coming to such a place, or to cry and wail, he must have been surprised. Mrs. Wright snapped, "Constable, you should be ashamed of yourself to keep such a cold, filthy jail! I never smelled such a smell in my life!"

"I'm sorry, ma'am," he mumbled. "I've been meaning to clean it up. Suppose I let Ben out and you can sit near the stove and talk. I'll leave you alone with him."

Nobody spoke as the constable opened the cell door with his massive iron key. He left, closing the jail door after him.

Mrs. Wright did go to pieces then. Ben quickly took her in his arms, and she sobbed against him while he patted her back. "This isn't the end of the world, mother," he said soothingly. "This isn't so terrible."

Jess studied his brother. He had expected him to be changed. After all, no member of the family had ever been in jail before, and wasn't it natural that such an experience would change a person? No, Ben looked just the same. He and Jess both had their father's sandy hair and blue eyes, but Ben was the tallest of the three. Now his head almost touched the ceiling of the low-raftered room.

He gently let his mother go. "Ma, where's the food you brought me?" he demanded cheerfully. "I'm starved."

"Didn't the sheriff's wife feed you?" Mr. Wright asked.

"Yes," Ben told him, "but no woman in Jericho cooks as well as Ma. I saved my appetite until you came."

His mother spread a clean napkin on the desk, then laid

20

out china and silver. Ben went to work on the fried chicken and homemade bread. "You brought enough for an army," he joked.

"When do they say the trial will be?" his father asked.

"Tomorrow, likely. The circuit judge comes then."

"We'll have to get a lawyer, but there isn't one in Jericho. I'll send to Smithtown for one."

"Why do we need to go to the expense of hiring a lawyer?" Ben asked. "The facts are clear enough. I was caught red-handed with two slaves hidden in the back of the wagon. We can't change the facts. It's only a question of how big the fine will be and whether we can raise it. If we can't, then I'll work out the fine after I serve the prison sentence."

Mrs. Wright suddenly sat down. The cool way Ben talked about it only made the situation seem more grim and real. Her eyes were dull with unhappiness, but she said nothing.

"We'll raise the fine," her husband said confidently. "We could get a mortgage on the farm, but we probably won't have to. Mr. Fuller came to the house last night and said that others in the movement want to help. I won't feel badly if we have to take their money. They feel it was only bad luck that you were caught and not them."

"All right, so that's that, and we don't need to talk about it any more," Ben said. He cut the pumpkin pie and took a big wedge. He went on, "At least the county prison will be cleaner than this one. Do you know what worried me most last night? It wasn't the fact of being in jail. It was what Ma would say if I came home and brought a mess of bedbugs in my clothes!"

The men laughed, but Mrs. Wright cried indignantly, "Bedbugs! It's high time the women in this town learned what a terrible place this is, and I'm going to tell them!"

21

"Now your mother has a new cause to work for," Mr. Wright told the boys.

They talked no more of jail or the trial. Ben wanted to know how things were going at home. "You've got quite a job cut out for yourself, fellow," he told Jess, "with my work and yours too."

"Jess wants to take your place in the underground," Mr. Wright mentioned.

Ben said sharply, "I hope you said, 'No.' Jess is too young."

"Your mother wouldn't listen to it, and I felt the same way," Mr. Wright told him. "There's enough work on the farm for the boy to do. Besides that, we've got to fix up an inside shelter for the poor souls who'll come needing help."

"I wondered about that," Ben said, "whether you intended to go on or planned to drop out."

"We won't give up the work," his father said. "Our station is the only one between Smithtown and Holden. We have to keep it open. We have no real choice."

"Good," Ben said with satisfaction. "I hoped you'd decide that way. The fact I got caught doesn't change the rightness of the cause."

It was time to leave. "I'll be in court tomorrow," Mr. Wright promised, "but I'm not bringing your mother or Jess. As soon as you're settled in the county jail at Holden, I'll bring them up to see you."

The constable came in then. "If your folks are leaving, I'll have to put you back in the cell, Ben," he apologized.

Ben's sense of humor didn't fail him now. "Don't worry about me, folks," he called after his family. "While you're all working hard doing my chores, I'll be enjoying a nice, lazy vacation."

CHAPTER THREE

THAT EVENING the thermometer dropped to ten above. When supper was over, Mr. Wright announced that a new shelter must be fixed immediately. "We can't risk the chance Eben Fuller will bring people before it's ready," he said. "It would be murder to put them in that hole under the barn floor. They'd freeze to death. Bring a lantern and come with me, Jess."

"What have you got in mind?" his wife asked.

"The smoke house ought to be a good place," he told her. Jess followed his father to the attic.

The house was a hundred years old, and before stoves were invented it had been heated by fireplaces, three on the first floor, one on the second. The huge chimney measured six feet each way, where it rose through the attic. In the olden days a small room had been built against it. A hole had been broken through the bricks to allow smoke from the downstairs fires to circulate. Here the hams and bacon had been hung to dry and smoke-cure.

This smoke house hadn't been used for many years. Sparks flying up the chimney could set fire to the attic. When Jess's father bought the house he bricked up the hole.

Jess helped his father pull away the accumulation of old newspapers, furniture, and books which had been piled against the door. It creaked open, and they caught the scent of smoke and cured hams, which had lingered all the time the room was closed. Mr. Wright held up the lantern.

The tiny, square room was festooned with heavy cobwebs. Mud hornets had plastered their nests on the walls. Soot and dirt lay an inch thick.

"It's lucky your mother didn't come up with us," Mr. Wright said. "She's such a cleanly woman, she'd be miserable to know there was any such rat's hole as this in her house. Take the lantern with you, and fetch the broom and dust pan and some scrapers to take off the mud nests."

"Father, we can't put people in such an awful place," Jess protested.

"It'll be all right once it's cleaned up. They'll be warm anyway from the heat coming up the chimney, and they'll be safe. I don't reckon they'll mind if it's dark and gloomy, as long as it's safe."

Jess brought the things his father wanted, and they went to work. It was one of the worst jobs Jess had ever tackled. They choked and coughed, working in a cloud of dust and soot. Jess started to carry the dirt down the stairs, but his father said, "We'll pitch it out the window and take care of it later." They pried off the fan-shaped window at the end of the attic and threw out the buckets of dirt.

Mrs. Wright came to the foot of the stairs. "What are you two doing?"

"We're cleaning out the smoke house, but don't you come a step nearer," her husband warned.

At last the worst of the mess was gone. Jess brought a pail of soapy water and rags and they washed down the rough walls and scrubbed the floor. "Now you can come," Mr. Wright called down to his wife.

24

They poked through the cast-off furniture and found a small bed, a rug for the floor, a couple of chairs. The place didn't look so bad, then. In fact, Jess realized that if he'd only thought to explore the smoke house before, he could have had a nice, private den of his own.

Mrs. Wright brought sheets and blankets and made up the bed. They left a lantern full of oil. "Aren't you afraid people might suffocate in here?" Jess asked.

"No," his father said. "These old houses are built kind of loose in the joints. Enough air circulates through the attic and around the door. If we're hiding fugitives and we get visitors of the wrong sort, meaning the sheriff or a marshal, then one of us will slip up and pile junk back against the door. Let's try that now. We have to make sure that the place looks as though nothing at all had been disturbed."

"We can't put back the cobwebs," Jess pointed out.

"No," his father said cheerfully, "but maybe we can hire some spiders to spin new ones."

When they piled back the boxes and furniture against the door, the place looked the same as it had before they opened up the smoke house.

The next day was Saturday. Jess was relieved that he didn't have to go to school. Whatever happened in town today, he'd have a couple of days to get used to it before he had to meet his schoolmates again. His father left, taking another basket of food and some books and heavy clothes for Ben.

The house seemed very quiet after he had gone. "How long do you suppose it'll be before Father gets back?" Jess wondered.

"There's no way of knowing," his mother said, and added, "We haven't had much experience with prisons and trials and sheriffs. Nobody in my family or your father's ever broke the law."

There was a note of bitterness in her voice Jess had never heard before. He didn't often have a chance to talk with either of his parents this way, about things that mattered, not just about the ordinary happenings of the farm. He said, "There's one thing that's not clear to me. How did Pa get into this work in the first place?"

"That happened about three months ago," she said. "Don't you remember? An abolitionist came down from Boston to hold a public meeting in Smithtown, and your father went. He was converted to the cause that night."

"Aren't the abolitionists the ones who want a law passed to set the slaves free right away?" Jess asked. "What's the matter with that idea?"

His mother was rolling out pie crust on a wooden board. He loved to watch the deft, neat way she did it. There was a bowl of sliced, dry apples on the table. Jess had a feeling that if he kept her talking it would take her mind off what was happening in town, and make the morning go faster. He perched on a stool and helped himself to the dried apples, which were dusted with sugar. "Why isn't that a good idea?" he insisted, "just to set all the slaves free?"

"It's not that simple," his mother told him. "A lot of cotton is raised in the South for the mills in the North and in England. The cotton farmers need slave help in the fields."

"But it's wrong!"

"Of course it's wrong. We know that and so do some good people in the South. There's a movement to buy the slaves and send them back to Africa to live . . ."

"Why isn't that another good idea?" Jess broke in.

"It's just hard to do, that's all. It's hard to raise enough money to buy the black men's freedom. It's difficult to get the Southerners to let them go, when cheap help is needed in the cotton fields."

Jess said stubbornly, "A thing that's as wrong as one man owning another ought to be changed, whether it's difficult or not."

She gave him a long look and sighed, "Jess, it's only because you're young that right and wrong look simple."

He supposed she couldn't help it, but Jess was getting very tired of being reminded how young he was. He changed the subject. "How many do get away through the underground?"

"Nobody knows. It's like a train system that doesn't have any tracks or trains. The underground is secret and hidden. There are routes through all the free states. They say a good many get to Canada by crossing over into Ohio. Your father's acquainted with men in New York state who have helped hundreds of fugitives. It was easier before this new slave law was passed. Many of the runaways used to settle down in the free states, once they got out of Dixie. Now, they're not safe anywhere in the North, and that's tragic. Thousands of them have found work and raised families and bought their own homes."

"Like the Cowells, in town," Jess pointed out.

"Yes, like the Cowells. But I understand they're getting very worried, and Mr. Cowell is thinking about leaving Connecticut and moving on, although he's lived here in peace and safety for ten years."

She was putting the top crusts on the pies, sealing the edges with a fork. "Jess, step outside and see if your father's coming," she suggested. "The longer he stays away the more worried I get. I know he'll come straight home after the trial. He won't keep us in suspense any longer than he has to."

Jess went out and listened. Often, on a still winter morning, he could hear a horse coming miles away on the main road between Jericho and Smithtown. His sharp ears caught the faraway beat of horses' hooves on the frozen road. "Somebody's coming," he called.

He waited for the buggy to come in sight, thinking, Maybe they let Ben off with a warning. Maybe there'll be two men in the buggy.

No, his father was alone. Jess caught Major's head strap. "How did it go?" he asked, while his father climbed down.

"I wish I had better news," Joseph Wright said heavily, "and yet it could be worse than it is. The judge might have given Ben six months in prison. He gave him only half of that and a five hundred dollar fine."

He went right to the house. Jess took off Major's harness and gave him a hasty rubdown, then followed.

His mother's face was wet with tears, but she had hold of herself. "Ninety days are a great many days, but they won't last forever," she said. "How are we going to raise the fine, though, Joe?"

"It's already done," her husband said. "I took the deed to the house with me, planning to take out a mortgage at the bank, but I didn't have to. Eben Fuller met me outside the court and handed me four hundred dollars in cash, which he and the Reverend Sykes had collected from friends in the underground. I took the other hundred out of the savings account."

"It won't hurt us to go another year with a leaky roof," his wife said. That precious hundred dollars had been saved up to pay for having the roof re-shingled in the spring.

"How was Ben?" Jess asked.

"Your brother seemed fine." Mr. Wright was living over the court trial in his mind. "Ben's quite a man," he said slowly. "The judge took over the questioning, after the federal man testified how he caught Ben with the runaways. The judge asked Ben, 'Do you admit you were breaking the law by transporting slaves?'

"Ben looked him right in the eye and said, 'It's not a question of admitting it, your honor. I never denied it. I'm only sorry I was caught. That's my only regret.'

"The judge asked, 'Would you do it again?'

" 'Yes, sir, I would and will, just as soon as I get out of prison,' Ben told him."

"I wonder if Ben wouldn't have gotten off with a lighter sentence, if he hadn't spoken out so boldly," Mrs. Wright said.

"I doubt it," her husband told her. "I couldn't help getting the impression the judge felt sympathetic to Ben.

"As you say, Viney, three months aren't forever. We'll get through them somehow."

The house seemed very quiet without Ben around. Ben had a gift of light-hearted laughter, which the others missed. Christmas was coming on, though, and they had to keep Christmas. Ben insisted on that.

In mid-December his family drove fifteen miles to Holden to see him at the county prison. Ben said, "I'll have a miserable day if I think you're not celebrating Christmas."

He gave them a list of things he wanted. In the short

29

time he'd been in prison, he had gotten to know many of the other inmates. He asked his father to buy small gifts for them.

Jess and his father climbed the hill behind the farm and cut a cedar and hauled it home. Mrs. Wright got out the paper ornaments she treasured from year to year, the silver and gold angels, and paper balls. They spent a pleasant evening stringing popcorn, to festoon the tree. Mr. Wright bought a pound of cranberries at the store, and they strung those to give the tree a bit of red.

They made a trip to town to do their shopping. Jess had saved his pennies and nickels all year. He bought his mother a lace collar he knew she wanted and a dozen red handkerchiefs for his father. His gift for Ben was a joke present, a file. His idea was that if Ben got bored with prison he could file his way through the bars. His parents bought Ben some warm wool clothes.

Two days before Christmas they went to Holden again. A foot of new snow had fallen, so they drove the sleigh. Regardless of the fact that this was a very grim occasion —the first time the family had ever been separated on a holiday—Jess couldn't keep his spirits down. The snow sang under the runners, Major's harness bells jingled, and Major was bursting with energy to be out and running on the clean, packed snow.

They visited with Ben in the county sheriff's office and gave him his gifts and those for his prison friends. Ben chattered cheerfully, and his mother kept back her tears. They didn't speak of serious things.

On the ride home, Jess and his parents didn't talk much. Mrs. Wright was quiet, and her men, respecting her feelings, were gentle with her. Mr. Wright did say, as they turned in their own lane at dusk, "I've been proud of my family many times, but I doubt if I'll ever be prouder than I was today."

It had been a long, exhausting day. They ate the hot soup Mrs. Wright dished up for them. Then Jess's father suggested, "You'd better wash up, son, and go right to bed."

Mrs. Wright reminded him, "I'll have to have firewood for the morning. Let Jess fetch that first."

Jess was pulling on his coat when a knock came at the door. It wasn't an ordinary banging; it was two soft knocks, then a pause, then three.

Mrs. Wright's hand flew to her heart. Her husband said, "Open the door, Jess."

Jess slid back the bolt. A man and a woman stood on the threshold, their eyes gleaming, blinking in the light. The Negro woman held a baby in her arms.

CHAPTER FOUR

She stumbled into the brightly lit kitchen and started to fall. Her husband caught her. "Are we expected?" he asked. "Is this the right place?"

Jess's mother took the woman from him and led her to a chair. "Yes, this is the right place."

"Thank you, madam." The tall, slim Negro didn't sound like anyone Jess had ever heard before. His speech was precise and careful. He was dark brown and handsome, with neat features. The woman was smaller and gleaming black. Jess couldn't see the baby, for the blanket was tightly wrapped around it.

Mr. Wright quickly pulled the curtains across the windows and bolted the door. "How did you get here?" he asked.

"A man who didn't give his name brought us and left us at the end of your road, sir. He heard a horseman coming behind, and let us out quickly."

"Where do you come from?"

"From South Carolina, sir."

"No, I mean originally. You don't sound like anyone else who's passed through here."

"I'm from Jamaica. I'm a free citizen under the British crown, but I have no papers to prove that. So I have no more rights than any Negro in the South."

"Well, that explains your English manner of speech."

The woman kept glancing from one to another, clutching her baby as though she was ready to run. Mrs. Wright warmed the soup and served the newcomers. Then she asked the woman, "Won't you let me take your baby and give him some milk while you eat?"

"Martha, let the lady take him," the man ordered. His wife reluctantly gave up the child.

Mrs. Wright laid back the blanket. "What a beautiful little boy," she murmured. He gulped the milk, watching her with big, brown eyes.

"Have you had a hard trip?" Jess asked.

"Yes, sir, we have," the man told him, "it's been very hard. The man with a red beard who brought us here said it might be easier from here on. He didn't give his name."

"We've found it's better for people who come by way of the underground not to learn last names," Mr. Wright explained. "If they don't know them, they can't give information in case they're caught. I'm Joseph, and my wife is Lavinia, and this tall lad is our son, Jess."

"I'm called John. That gentleman told us about your older son going to prison for helping people like us." John choked, and his eyes filled with tears. "Forgive me," he murmured. "I'm more tired than I realized. The kindness of the people who help us is wonderful, but when we learn what it can cost you, that's hard to bear."

"What you need now is a night's sleep in a real bed. That'll put new life in you," Mr. Wright said.

The baby's tiny fist was waving aimlessly in the air. Jess touched it, and the velvet fingers seized his and clung.

The violence of his own feeling startled him. He felt a surge of hot hatred for the men who bought and sold helpless babies like this one. The others were looking at Jess curiously. "What's his name?" he asked.

35

"Peter," the baby's father told him.

"Do you want to hold him, Jess?" Mrs. Wright asked.

"No," Jess said, stepping back, "he might break." The others smiled.

Mr. Wright took charge. "We won't put these folks in the attic tonight. Let's give them the guest room, Viney. There's a cot there for the baby. If we lock the house tight, we'll have plenty of warning, in case anybody comes."

That was the beginning of a strange visit. The next day Mr. Wright rode north to Holden to find out if the man who ran the underground station there was ready to receive three passengers. When he returned he reported that the Holden station-master was away, having taken his family to visit relatives for the holiday. Mr. Wright had left word with the hired man, who could be trusted. The passengers would spend Christmas with the Wrights.

Two days was the longest they had ever kept runaways. A long visit seemed dangerous, but John and Martha couldn't continue their journey until the Holden agent was ready to take them north.

The house was kept locked at all times. John was posted at a window in the parlor to watch for strangers turning off the main road. Otherwise, life went on normally.

Martha bloomed in those few days. The terror that shadowed her dark eyes gradually disappeared. When she wasn't caring for the baby she followed Mrs. Wright around, her eyes full of love and gratitude. She took over some of the Christmas cooking, making cakes and cookies she had learned to bake in the kitchen of the Southern family where she had been a slave. Her husband had been a butler in that same house.

They had no tales to tell of cruelty on that plantation;

36

the people who had owned them had been reasonably kind. John, however, who had known freedom, was determined that his wife and son should live free, that Martha should lose her fear of people with white skins.

Visitors came only once, and that was on Christmas Eve. John left his post at the front window and hurried his family to the smoke house in the attic. Jess went with them, to disguise the hiding place. When he came down, though, he found that the visitors were only Sven Swanson's family, from the next farm. The Wrights and the Swansons always got together during the holiday, to exchange small presents and share a little party of coffee and cake.

Mrs. Swanson had knitted a beautiful sweater for Ben. "I wanted to do something for him," this kind neighbor said. "We love and admire your son."

Sven's sisters busied themselves tying Swedish decorations on the tree in the parlor. Jess was tongue-tied with Sven. He longed to tell him that at that very moment fugitives were hiding in the attic. He didn't even give a hint. This underground business was far too serious for him to take the chance, even with a good friend like Sven.

Mr. Swanson brought up the subject, though, when they were all sitting around the kitchen table. "Have there been any more abolitionist meetings, Joe?"

"Not lately," Jess's father told him.

"When there is one, I'd like to go. I want to find out more about this work you're doing."

"I'm glad you feel that way, Oscar, and I'll let you know when there's a meeting," Mr. Wright promised.

When the neighbors were ready to leave, Jess and his parents went outside with them. Cheerful calls of "Merry Christmas!" rang through the clear night. "It's a fine thing to have such neighbors," Mrs. Wright said contentedly.

"Yes, and I'll be glad if Oscar Swanson decides he wants to help us," her husband added.

"I'd trust Sven," Jess put in.

His mother shivered in her heavy shawl but seemed in no hurry to go inside. "I never saw the stars so bright or so close. Christmas Eve ought to be a good night for seeing the Star of Bethlehem. Is there really such a star?"

"Give up your star-gazing and come in before you catch cold," her husband ordered with a chuckle.

He sent Jess to tell John and Martha that they could come down. Martha helped Mrs. Wright wash up the dishes. Joseph Wright suggested, "Come outside, John, and see what a beautiful night it is."

Jess went with them, for it was hard to stay indoors. It was a magical sort of a night. Fresh snow lay over the valley, the hills forming a great dark bowl. Lights flickered in farmhouses far away. Jess thought of the old fable that on Christmas Eve all the animals talked together, waiting in the barns to greet the Lord Jesus, if He came. The Wrights' cows and horses and pigs were silent in the dark barn, but the hens seemed restless, clucking and squawking. Probably it was only the moonlight, almost as bright as day, which disturbed them.

"John, maybe you know whether there's actually a Star of Bethlehem that we can see," Mr. Wright said.

The Jamaican was gazing into the northern sky. "No, I don't, sir, but I can see the one I have to follow," he said. "Jess, do you see the North Star? To black people that's the only important star in the sky, for that's the one that guides them out of slavery and up to Canada. When my people are getting ready to escape, that's what we say. 'I'm taking the North Star.'" For a long time, John stood

38

gazing with strange intensity at that particular far beacon in the sky.

Christmas was a good day. Mrs. Wright had changed her gifts around so that the visitors had a share in the receiving. Jess suspected that the stockings she wrapped in tissue for John had been knit for himself, but that was all right. Martha received a new red flannel petticoat, and the baby was delighted with beads strung on stout string.

Instead of ignoring the fact that Ben was not with them, they all spoke of him often and lovingly. Tired out by the long, happy day, they went to bed early.

A knocking awoke them. Jess saw by the moon's position in the sky that it must be nearly morning. He pulled aside his curtain, and saw a wagon loaded with hay in the yard, and guessed who it was. The underground agent in Holden had gotten the message that passengers were waiting in Jericho and had come to take them on to the next station.

Jess went down and let him in. He was astonished, for this Holden agent was a wizened old man, white-haired, blue-eyed, probably in his eighties. He seemed lively as a boy, though, the way he hopped down from the wagon seat.

His passengers hastily dressed. Martha cried steadily, while Mrs. Wright served them and the Holden man a hot breakfast. "Please, can't we stay here?" Martha begged. "I'd work my fingers to the bone for you folks!"

"No," her husband said firmly, "don't beg, Martha. We have to go on. Our son is going to be raised in freedom."

Jess's mother fed the baby and wrapped him in a new blanket she had made for him. The tears slid down her face too, and Jess guessed it was the baby she found hardest to let go.

The Wrights went out to see them off. The little family was bundled up in quilts on the seat with the Holden agent. When daylight came, he would hide them in the hay that filled the back of the wagon.

"When you reach Canada, send us a letter. We'll be anxious to hear," Mr. Wright instructed.

"I'd like to do that, but how can I when I don't know your last name, sir?" John asked.

Jess's father shook his hand. "I'll trust you with it, friend. The name is Wright."

"If we could only find the words to thank you . . ."

"There's no need. Take care of that little fellow. Be a good girl, Martha."

The old man clucked to the horses, and the fugitives were on their way. Jess and his parents watched until the wagon vanished into the night.

With Christmas over, life returned to normal. Jess and his mother cleaned the smoke house and changed the bedding, getting ready for the next visitors. Jess went to school but worked long hours at home. The chores were heavy for him and his father, without Ben's help.

One Sunday early in January when the roads were clear, they went to church for the first time since Ben's arrest. Mrs. Wright had been wanting to go, but bad weather had kept them home.

As soon as they sat down, Jess began to feel uncomfortable. Every time he glanced around, during the service, people were looking at the pew where the Wrights were.

The church was Jericho's social center. After the service, people always stood around and exchanged news and gossip. When Jess and his parents walked out of church, the Reverend Mills greeted them heartily at the door and inquired after Ben. Some of the townspeople stopped to speak, as they lingered on the steps. Others went on with a hasty, "Morning, Joseph, Lavinia." A few looked the other way, deliberately ignoring them.

Mrs. Wright's face was stiff and pale as she took her husband's arm and they walked to the long carriage shed behind the church were Major was tethered. Jess helped her up. The congregation was still coming out, and many stared openly as Mr. Wright swung Major into Main Street and set off at a fast clip. "What's the matter, Viney?" he asked.

"Nothing, Joseph."

"Are you upset by the way some folks acted?"

"Please, let's not talk about it."

They were all silent for a while, thinking deeply. They were halfway home when Mr. Wright asked, "Why didn't you go to the Ladies' Society Christmas party, Viney?"

"I wasn't asked," she said in a low voice.

Her husband began to sound angry. "You didn't have to be asked. You're secretary of it, aren't you?"

"I don't even know when it was," she said. "They didn't ask me to help. I've sent in my resignation."

"Why didn't you tell me this before?" he demanded.

"Because you've got enough on your mind, Joe, without worrying about a lot of silly women and their silly party."

"But when the women in town got together and decided to have a sewing club, you were one of those who organized it. They can't act this way!"

"They can, and they did," she said. "Don't get your dander up, Joe. We thought they were our friends, the people in church, the ladies in the club, and some are, don't forget that. Some still are. The others don't matter.

41

The minister is sympathetic. That's clear from the way he asked after Ben. But I suppose a few feel they can't afford to be friends now, because our son is in prison."

"Oh, Viney," he groaned, "I never realized what it could do to you when I took up this work."

"I promise I won't let it bother me," she said firmly. "The true friends won't stop being friends, even if they don't agree with what we do. The false friends we can do without."

Mr. Wright turned to Jess. "Is it this way with you at school?"

"No, it's not too bad," Jess told him. "Mr. House explained in history class about slavery and the underground, and that helped. Some of them look at me as though I was some kind of freak, but that doesn't bother me much."

"Sven is a good friend. He hasn't changed."

"No," Jess said. "The only trouble I have with him is that he keeps hinting he wants to help."

In the deep of winter, not many callers came to the farm. That very afternoon, though, one dropped in. Jess and his father had changed out of their Sunday clothes and were cleaning and mending harness in the barn. Sheriff Hodgkins tied his horse at the rail by the horse trough. Mrs. Wright must have seen him, for she called from the door, "George Hodgkins, if you want to come in out of the cold and have a cup of coffee, you're welcome."

"Thank you, Lavinia," he called back.

"Let's all go in," Mr. Wright suggested.

The sheriff came right to the point, when they were all gathered around the kitchen stove. "I saw you folks leave church this morning," he said. "You drove away as though you'd been shot out of a gun, Joe."

42

"I'm getting sick and tired of having people look down their noses at me and mine," Mr. Wright growled.

"You brought it on yourself," the sheriff said frankly. "You and Lavinia and I have been friends since we were knee high, Joe, but you're putting quite a strain on that friendship. How do you think I felt, having to lock your boy up?"

"You were forced into that by the federal man. We don't hold it against you," Jess's mother put in.

"Lavinia, can't you persuade Joe to give this up?" the sheriff asked. "How do I know he isn't continuing to break the law? How do I know you're not hiding slaves in this house this very minute? People in town think the Negroes are still passing through. I've told them that Joe Wright isn't mixed up in that business any longer, but, actually, I'm not certain at all."

Mr. Wright grinned. "Put your mind at ease, George. You're not under the roof with any fugitives."

"How do I know you won't help them, though, if any do come?"

"You don't."

The sheriff rose to his feet and banged on the table, so that the dishes jumped. "Joe, you've got to give me your word you won't break the law again!"

"Cool down, George," Mr. Wright ordered. "I'm not giving you my word. I'm not promising you anything. The law as it stands is wicked and inhumane, you know it."

The sheriff didn't answer.

"Don't you know that it's a bad law?" Mr. Wright insisted.

Mr. Hodgkins was getting angry again. "What makes you think you can decide which laws you'll obey and which you'll disobey?"

43

"In this case I can. Sometimes, a man's conscience comes before the law."

"What's going to happen if I ride into your yard some day with a warrant for your arrest?"

"I'll get into your buggy and ride to jail with you without making a fuss," Mr. Wright promised.

"And leave a kid like Jess here to run the farm alone?"

"Jess is in this with us," Mr. Wright said. "He feels as we do."

The sheriff glared angrily at each of them. Then he relaxed, and his hearty laugh boomed out. "You're the coolest bunch of crooks I've ever had to deal with since I was elected to office," he said cheerfully.

He picked up his hat. "I'm sorry you and your boys are tied up with a renegade like Joe, Lavinia. You're a nice woman and just as good-looking as you were when you were a girl, and you're still the best cook in Jericho. Thanks for the refreshments."

He climbed onto his horse while Jess held its head. "At least, friends, do me one favor," was his parting request. "Use some sense, and try not to make me catch you!"

CHAPTER FIVE

In mid-january the weather stayed clear and cold for several days. Jess had to miss a week of school to stay home and help his father manure the fields. This was his hard luck, for he would have to make up his lessons as best he could. It wasn't unusual, though. All the boys and girls at Pumpkin Hollow School came from farms and were often kept home when they were needed.

If there was one job Jess hated it was manuring, but he couldn't get out of it. The land had to be fed if it was going to yield good crops. Winter was the time to do it, when the snow was on the ground.

Filling the wagon with the heavy manure from the pile behind the barn was a back-breaking job. With a full load, his father drove over the fields. Jess stood in back and scattered the stuff.

After a couple of days at this job, both Jess and his father grew tired and irritable. It seemed as though life was too grubby to bear. They fell into bed at night exhausted, with nothing to look forward to but another day of the same hard labor. Jess couldn't help resenting it. He even envied Ben, who was lounging idly in a warm prison while he himself struggled to do Ben's work.

His mother watched him worriedly. "You're looking peaked," she said. "Maybe you're growing too fast. A boy

45

loses his strength when he shoots up too fast. Joseph, couldn't we hire somebody to help until the manuring is done?"

Mr. Wright didn't answer, and Jess guessed why. His father couldn't afford to hire a man. The hundred dollars he had paid for Ben's fine had wiped out the family's savings. Jess said, "No, Ma, we don't need to hire anybody. Pa and I can manage. Sure I'm tired, but so is Pa. We'll be through in a few days."

The grateful look his father gave him for understanding the problem was reward enough. When they went to the fields and were silently working together, Jess was glad he'd spoken up. What if he'd whined or let on he was sick or something to get out of it? He'd have a hard time, after that, convincing anybody he deserved to be treated as an adult.

They slept like logs at night during that hard time. Jess's room was at the back of the house. That was why he was the one who was awakened one night by a knocking on the door.

He lay and listened. It came again—two knocks, then three—the signal of the undergrounders. Dazed with sleep, Jess staggered out of bed and called softly from the window, "We'll be right down." He went to awaken his parents.

He got downstairs first and opened the kitchen door. He hadn't realized it was raining. Two entered, water dripping from their clothes. One was Mr. Fuller, the Smithtown agent, the other a thin, shivering Negro boy, about Ben's age.

Jess's parents appeared just as he was helping the boy out of his ragged coat. Mrs. Wright took in the situation at a glance. As always, her first thought was of food. Soup was kept ready, on the back of the stove. She bustled around, setting out dishes.

"This is Bart," Mr. Fuller said. "I'm afraid he's a mighty sick lad."

"You shouldn't have brought him out on a night like this!" Mrs. Wright exclaimed.

"I had no choice," the Smithtown agent told her. "He's in real trouble."

The boy had cowered away, trying to keep in the shadows. Mrs. Wright wasn't in the habit of taking any nonsense from young people or sick people. She led him to the rocker near the stove, pushed him into it, and put a bowl of hot soup in his hands. "You eat that," she ordered. "Every drop of it. Now."

"What kind of trouble is he in?" Mr. Wright asked. "Eben, you'd better tell us."

"He's too scared and sick to give a rational account," Mr. Fuller said, "but I got some of it from the man who brought him to my house. He must have come from one of the really bad plantations, somewhere in Virginia. A lot of the slaves on that place had tried to get away, because the overseer was a brute. The owner kept dogs for tracking runaways, and these dogs killed Bart's father. Bart saw it and went kind of crazy, took a hoe, and clubbed three hounds to death. The overseer found out who killed the dogs, and after that the boy had no choice except to run off. He knew he'd die if he stayed.

"He got as far as Philadelphia, and there by the mercy of God he fell into the hands of some Quakers. They hurried him north, for they got word that the overseer had sworn to catch him and was on his trail.

"An advertisement appeared in the New York papers, printing a full description of Bart, stating that he was a

47

dangerous maniac. The man who was hiding him there brought him to me yesterday. We don't dare take any chances on this one. We can't waste time getting him into Canada."

Jess's mother put her hand on Bart's forehead. "He's burning with fever!"

"That's what I was afraid of," Mr. Fuller said. "He picked up a cold. Maybe it's turned into pneumonia."

"We'll get him into bed right away," Mrs. Wright said. "Take him upstairs, Jess."

Obediently, the boy got up. He looked dazed and lost. Jess felt sick, seeing the fear and hopelessness in his eyes. He took Bart's arm. "What bed shall I put him in, Ma?"

"You'll put him in the safest hiding place you've got," Mr. Fuller said grimly. "He'll stay here the rest of this night and tomorrow. Tomorrow night, Joe, as soon as it's dark you'll have to take him on to Holden."

"Can't we fix a cot for him down here near the stove?" Mrs. Wright asked. "He's got to be kept warm, and he's got to be looked after."

"No," Mr. Fuller said, "hide him."

"Do as Eben says, Lavinia," Mr. Wright warned.

She was still grumbling and fussing as she followed Jess and the strange boy to the attic. She piled extra quilts on the bed, then went to fix a dose of medicine to bring down the fever. Jess undressed Bart and covered him.

Bart's eyes closed, and he shuddered with chills. Jess sat with him until his mother came back, then supported his head to help him swallow the medicine.

The sick boy's head fell back weakly, but when Mrs. Wright suggested, "Let's leave him and let him sleep, Jess," he roused up.

"Please don't lock me in," he begged.

48

"We have to, for your own safety," Mrs. Wright said gently.

"Please, please leave the door open!"

"He wants to be able to run," Jess guessed.

Mrs. Wright sounded as though she was addressing a small child. "You're not to be afraid, Bart. We won't let anyone near you to take you away. Nobody is coming with dogs or whips here. You're sick, so you've got to rest and get strong. We're going to leave the lamp for you, so you won't be in the dark, but we'll close the door and hide where it is. Before anyone can get to you, he'll have to break into the house and then get past my husband and my son. That can't be done. Go to sleep now."

Bart's eyes had looked kind of crazy with fear. Now it was wonderful to see how the reason came into them. He turned his head, and almost immediately his heavy breathing showed he was asleep.

Mr. Fuller was getting ready to leave, when they came down. Mrs. Wright sounded sick and angry at the same time as she said, "He'll have to stay with us at least a week, Mr. Fuller. I've seen pneumonia before, and I know his life depends on his getting rest and proper food."

"I appreciate how you feel, Mrs. Wright, but the answer is 'No,'" Mr. Fuller said. "Bart leaves here tomorrow night."

"But he can't travel in this weather! He'll die!"

"He's got to take that chance and so do we. Your husband will tell you the same thing."

"It's true, Lavinia," Jess's father said. "The boy is a threat to the whole underground system. If he's caught, it might wipe out this whole branch of the railroad. It's not his fault, God knows, for he's the most pitiful case we've

51

seen yet. But apparently his owner is a rich man who can hire any number of detectives to track him down, and we have to believe he'll do exactly that. He can't afford to have this boy escape. Bart has to be taken back and punished. Otherwise, every slave on that plantation will move heaven and earth to get away. That master has to get Bart back as an example to the others, so their mortal fear of him and his overseer won't be weakened."

Jess's mother sank into the rocker, put her hands over her face, and sobbed. It was Mr. Fuller who went to her to comfort her. "Mrs. Wright, this is how it is, with no prettying up," he said. "You're a strong, wise woman, so the ugliness of this awful business won't break you. Men like your husband and me have to be hard. If we let you have your way and Bart is caught, the route he took might be traced back to where he first met those Quakers. Then this branch of the railroad would be closed to all the poor souls who might have used it to escape to Canada.

"That's the harsh truth of the situation. If Bart dies, then that will be a tragedy. But if the route is wrecked for all the others who might have come after him, that would be a bigger tragedy."

All that day Jess's mother worked without ceasing over the desperately ill Negro, making mustard poultices for his chest, feeding him hot food, concocting doses of medicine. When she wasn't working over him she sat beside him, her hand in his, trying to put some of her own faith and strength into him. He understood when she prayed, and his lips moved, repeating the words. Otherwise, he lay motionless, sunk in his own dark, terrible memories.

Jess went with his father to the fields, but kept going back to the house to learn if there was any change in

52

Bart's condition. Mr. Wright was silent and grim. Jess was struggling to suppress his own anger. Some of it was against his father.

His mother had begged her husband to fetch Dr. Gray from town, and Jess had added his own pleas, but Mr. Wright had refused. "It's better to take the chance the boy will die than let the doctor know he's here," he explained. "None of us know how Dr. Gray feels about slavery. He might doctor the boy, then turn him over to the sheriff."

Jess worked with savage intensity, shoveling manure until the muscles of his back and arms were stiff with agonizing pain.

Dark came at five o'clock, and Mr. Wright ordered Jess to harness Major to the buggy. It had curtains, and would be warmer than the wagon. Ignoring his wife's "Please, Joe!" he went himself to bring Bart down.

He was gentleness itself with the sick boy. "I'm sorry, lad, but it's time to go," he said. He and Jess dressed him, and Mr. Wright put his best wool shirt on the runaway. They half carried him downstairs.

Jess wrapped the blankets around him. "Pa, can't I come with you? Change your mind, and let me come," he begged.

"No, son. I'll manage. Stay, and take care of your mother."

The metal rims of the buggy's wheels struck sparks as it lurched down the frozen lane. Jess watched it out of sight. He was still filled with rage. Bart was gone, and they probably would never learn what happened to him.

Jess was thinking deeply. He himself had never known anything but a happy home, where there was warmth and food and love. What he knew now of one boy named Bart had given him a glimpse into a life that had been nothing but fear and want and pain. It seemed to Jess that the contrast was more than he could bear.

Why, why? was the question that tormented him. How could such injustice exist in a decent world? Why did he have everything, and Bart nothing?

His father returned home before daybreak. Jess and his mother were waiting, and to her questions Mr. Wright answered reassuringly, "The lad seemed a little better when I left him. He'll lay over in Holden for a day, and the people there will take as good care of him as you did, Viney. I think maybe he turned the corner and started to mend. I believe he'll make it to Montreal."

This was Friday, the day they were due to visit Ben. Mr. Wright was so tired, though, he confessed, "I can't face the trip. Major's worn out, too. Jess, go over and see if you can borrow the Swansons' mare. They'll be willing to lend her, so you can take your mother to see Ben."

Jess walked the mile to the next farm and found Mr. Swanson in the barn. Sven was at school. Mr. Swanson's face lit up with pleasure because Jess asked for the loan of his mare. "It's little enough to do," he said. "Any time your mother wants to see her boy, I'll drive her myself, or you can take my horse." He gave Jess a halter, and Jess rode the sorrel mare home bareback.

She was a beautiful little horse, a fast pacer, and despite the worry that laid so heavily on him, Jess couldn't help feeling more cheerful as he and his mother set out. Heated soapstones warmed their feet under the buffalo robe.

By tacit consent, he and his mother didn't discuss their troubles. Pink came into her cheeks. All the way to

54

Holden, she told stories of the days when she was a girl.

Jess put the mare into a trot when they entered Holden's main street. It occurred to him that he made quite a dashing figure. His mother sobered him though, for she said sadly, "Poor Bart is hidden in a house in this town, and we don't even know what house, or where."

The county jail was a square, brick building on a side street. Jess tied the horse at the rail in front, then took the basket of homecooked food. It was always a bad moment for his mother when she entered, smelling the jail odor, feeling the oppression of the place.

The county sheriff came to the door to greet them. "Your boy's not in his cell," he said. "I put him in my own office. He has a visitor." The sheriff gallantly conducted Mrs. Wright to the office.

"Why, Reverend Mills!" Mrs. Wright exclaimed. The minister of their own Jericho church was with Ben.

Ben jumped up and gave his mother a hearty hug and kiss. "Mr. Mills got so worried about the state of my soul, he drove all the way up here to check on it," he said gaily.

Mrs. Wright looked shocked, for she wasn't used to hearing anybody joking with the minister. The young man smiled. "I'm glad we came at the same time, Mrs. Wright. I intended to try to see your good husband tomorrow. I understand he is a friend of the Reverend Sykes, of Smithtown."

Mrs. Wright hesitated, and Jess knew why. She wasn't sure that Mr. Mills knew the Smithtown pastor was a member of the underground railroad.

"Mr. Sykes came to see me recently," Mr. Mills went on. "He has asked me to let an abolitionist speaker from Hartford use our church for a meeting in Jericho."

Ben asked, "And are you going to, pastor?"

"Yes. I hope your parents will help me arrange it."

Ben said, "That can hurt you with some of your own church people."

The young minister answered thoughtfully. "I'm aware of that, Ben. But I've been doing some serious thinking lately. I believe the time is coming when every man will have to stand up and be counted. If the ministers want to be real leaders in their towns, they'll have to make up their minds soon on which side they want to be counted in this question of slavery."

CHAPTER SIX

THE MINISTER soon left, to give Mrs. Wright and Jess time alone with Ben. Ben was jubilant. "Pa will be pleased," he said. "The undergrounders will have an easier time if the attitude of the public can be changed. Confound it, I wish I could get out of this jail to be at the meeting!"

"I'm glad you can't!" his mother exclaimed. "It'll be hard enough, without a firebrand like you stirring things up!" Then she realized she had said she was glad her son was in prison and had to laugh at herself.

On the way home, though, she was thoughtful. Usually, leaving Ben behind made her sad. Today she was more concerned about the minister. Jess echoed what Ben had said, that the abolitionist meeting might help the underground. His mother said, "Yes, but it might hurt Mr. Mills himself. He's a good man and has a promising career ahead of him. Also, he has a wife and small children to support. If the church people go against him in this matter, it could hurt his career."

Mr. Wright agreed with her when he heard about the meeting, but he was delighted that the minister was coming out publicly against slavery. "When right and wrong are as clear as they are in this issue," he said, "the clergymen have got to stick their necks out, if they're any kind of leaders."

"It's a very valuable neck Mr. Mills is sticking out," his wife reminded him. "He has more at stake than simple people like us."

Mr. Wright took the pastor to Smithtown to talk with the Reverend Sykes. When he came home, he reported, "Everything is set. The meeting will be at the church two weeks from tonight. The speaker is a minister from one of the churches in Hartford."

"Has Mr. Mills consulted with any of the other members of our Board of Elders besides you?" Mrs. Wright asked.

"No," her husband said, "and he isn't going to. The vote might go against him, and that would stop the meeting from ever taking place. Mr. Sykes advised it was better to take a chance and go ahead and hold it."

He grew increasingly nervous as the days went by. His fear was that no one would attend, or that a snowstorm would prevent the meeting, or that the church leaders would get together and take a stand against letting an abolitionist speak in the church.

He needn't have worried. When the big night came, the winter sky was clear. Buggies and wagons and traps of every kind were converging on the church, when the Wrights arrived. Mr. Wright had a hard time finding a place to tie Major, for every hitching post along Main Street was taken.

Jess and his parents joined the crowd at the door. Lamps lit the church. The pews were rapidly filling. The Reverend Sykes sat up front, beside a small, gray man whom Jess assumed was the Hartford abolitionist.

Mr. Sykes glimpsed tall Joseph Wright towering over

58

the crowd and made his way to him. "Come up front and sit with us, Joe," he ordered.

"No, thanks," Mr. Wright said firmly. "I'm too famous, or infamous, in this town already. I'll stay with my family."

The room was unheated, save for one huge stove in the middle. This glowed red with a roaring fire, but only those who had come early to sit near it got any benefit from it. As the crowd kept pressing in, the place warmed up, though. Soon every pew was taken. People stood in the back.

Jess glanced at his mother's tense face. The hall was filled with men; only a handful of women had come. Jess had noticed that only a few of these had greeted his mother warmly. Some had stared at her indignantly.

The lamps along the walls gave only a flickering light. Jess made out a group in back and recognized Tom Slaney, Sim's father, with other rough characters who were talking and laughing loudly. The Snake Mountain gang had come. Why? Jess knew with a shiver they could only have come to make trouble.

The regular churchgoers glared angrily at these invaders. Mountain people rarely ventured inside the church. No wonder they didn't know how to behave.

People stopped talking and moving about, for the Reverend Mills had stepped up to the pulpit. Jess saw how pale and serious the young minister was as he began, "Thank you, good people, for coming out on a cold night to listen to this talk. Whether we agree or disagree with the issues which will be discussed, we all ought to be informed. With every passing day, the problem of slavery grows more critical in our beloved country. I am not up here to say what I think, though. I want to introduce the

Reverend Brown Willis of Hartford, who has made this long journey to speak to us. Let's hear him out. Afterwards, we can state our own views."

A voice from the back of the church boomed, "Let's not hear him out, let's throw him out!"

Everyone turned. Tom Slaney was grinning like an ape, pleased with his own cleverness. His gang took up the refrain, "Yes, let's throw him out!"

The minister's voice was calm, but it carried. "Unless we can show respect for a minister of the Lord in the Lord's own house, then this meeting will be adjourned before it begins. If you men back there cannot behave, then leave now."

Nobody moved. Mr. Slaney looked around, saw that his followers weren't going to back him up and subsided.

The Reverend Brown Willis came forward. He was so slight, he could hardly be seen over the pulpit, and so colorless and nondescript, Jess's heart sank. This meeting needed a strong man and a good speaker to keep control.

Mr. Willis began, and his voice, dry and monotonous, matched his appearance. He said he was glad to be there, and glad so many had come to hear him, and thanked Mr. Sykes and Mr. Mills for arranging the meeting. Then he paused.

When he began again, his face lit up with enthusiasm, and his voice rang out and filled the church. He actually seemed to grow in height. "We wonder what slavery is," he said. "None of us gathered here tonight know what slavery is. We breathe free air and we are our own masters. We cannot conceive what it is like, to breathe fear into our lungs with every breath we draw.

"Let's go back, to see how this wicked thing started. Two hundred years ago, ships began bringing Africans to

our shores. Most of these Africans were unloaded in Southern ports, and there they were sold. Only a few were brought at first. Then, a hundred years ago, the trickle turned into a flood. The ships that brought these poor blacks were Yankee ships, sailing under New England captains. The North, especially New England, has a heavy load of guilt to bear in this affair, for many of its families grew rich in this hellish trade.

"The blacks were sold and made to work like animals. But they are not animals. They are men and women whose skins happen to be dark.

"They have souls. Bear this in mind. Under their thin, black skins, their blood courses like ours, their nerves long for peace, their brains think. Their hearts long for kindness and justice and free air to breathe.

"Tonight, I ask you good people to think black. Think how it must be to be black, and so the easy prey of any man rich enough and powerful enough to hold you in bondage. Think how it must be to feel the whips laid on your back so heavily the blood runs, and not be allowed to cry out in protest. Think how a man must hate when he sees his wife and children at the mercy of brutes and cannot raise his hand or voice in their defense but must submit and say nothing."

The speaker paused, as though his thoughts were too dark for him to put them into words. He said slowly, "So, when pressed too hard, the slaves run away. This is an honorable tradition for men in bondage to run from their owners. In Roman days, Spartacus inspired his fellow slaves to defy their Roman masters. In Old Testament days, Moses led his fellow Jews out of bondage in Egypt.

"Now, in this country, though they have no leaders, black slaves are fleeing from their American masters.

63

They flee singly, in families, in small groups. There is only one guide for them, their North Star, which leads them as the fire led Moses in the desert.

"They have heard rumors where they should go, to Philadelphia, to Cincinnati, anywhere across the Mason-Dixon line which divides these United States into two countries—one slave, one free. They meet the first agent of the underground railroad, and he is kind. He binds the slave's wounds, gives milk to his baby, and wraps his wife in a warm shawl because she and her child could freeze to death in the cold northern winter.

"The agent hurries them on. He has to, for the Southern masters have their underground too, of slave-catchers who spread a filthy net over the North. These runaways are worth cash, remember that. The man may be worth as much as two thousand dollars, his wife another thousand; even his baby's value is reckoned in hundreds of dollars by men who buy human flesh.

"From house to house they go, hidden during the day in haylofts, in cellars, in attics, in caves, in holes in the ground. They are silent people, for they are listening for the footfall of the slave catcher. Night comes, and if they are lucky it is a friend who whispers, 'Come out, you have to travel now.' If their luck has run out, it is the sheriff, the professional slave catcher, the United States marshal; and they come out from their hiding place to look down the barrel of a gun. Then the chains are forged on their wrists and ankles, and they are carried helplessly away."

Again the speaker paused. There wasn't a sound in the church. Everyone bent forward, listening intently. But Jess saw, chilled, that some faces were rigid in expressions of anger and indignation.

Mr. Willis's voice now was matter of fact. "I ask you to

help these people. You are Americans. You live freely under a Bill of Rights that guarantees to everyone within our borders 'life, liberty, and the pursuit of happiness.' Help these people to live free, too. They are God's children like yourselves.

"My good friends, we of the underground don't want your money. We want your courage. We hold out a welcome to the stout-hearted. The day will come when all men, black, white, brown, yellow, and red, will live safely together under the laws of the United States. Until that time comes, though, we of the underground need you to join us in defying the federal law that sets at naught the law of God.

"We undergrounders find happiness in what we do, dangerous as it is. The poet Shakespeare expressed the way we feel. 'We few, we happy few, we band of brothers.' "

Mr. Willis raised his hand in a gesture of benediction. "Join with us, friends. Join our band of brothers."

Jess glanced along the row where he sat. His father, his arms folded, looked thoughtful, but it was his mother's expression that caught Jess's attention. Her face was alight with joy and excitement, and for a wild moment Jess thought she was going to stand up and cry out, "Yes, join us, join with us!"

She was too shy to do that, to speak out in public meeting, but she turned and caught her son's glance, and her smile was radiant.

If the gang from Snake Mountain had come to the meeting to break it up, they had changed their minds. They had left without starting trouble. The audience quietly filed out. Their own minister was at the door, as always, to shake hands with each one. The Reverend Mills looked hopeful and happy and asked Jess's father, "How do you think it went, Joe?"

Mr. Wright began, "I don't know——"

Ephraim Woods, who was the first elder of the church, who was the president of Jericho's bank, whom everyone looked up to because he was powerful and rich, had come up behind the Wrights. His voice cut across what Joe Wright had started to say. The minister put out his hand, but Mr. Woods ignored it. His stony face was one that Jess had noticed during the speaking. "I want a meeting of the church elders," he said coldly. "Will you call it, Reverend Mills, or shall I?"

The crowd stopped moving and listened. The minister said, "If you want a meeting, Mr. Woods, I will call it. When do you wish it?"

"Soon," Mr. Woods said. "No later than next week. This dangerous nonsense must be stopped at once."

Jess's father's voice had an edge to it, as he asked courteously, "You'll let all the elders know, won't you, Reverend Mills, when such a meeting is to take place?"

The chairman of the Board of Elders spoke for the minister. "I know you're on the Board, Joe Wright, but we won't need you at the meeting. You won't be welcome."

"I am an elected member of the Board of this church," Mr. Wright said, his tone icy. "Until I resign and another man is elected in my place, I shall come to all meetings and vote on all questions. I'll be there."

The crowd parted then, and Joe Wright strode down the steps.

Tom Slaney and his men were waiting outside on the lawn, not far off. Tom sang out, "I suppose you think you're a big man now, Joe Wright. Well, you and your jailbird son are no better than the rest of us. Maybe you need to be taken down a peg!"

Mrs. Wright took her husband's arm and tried to urge him away. Maybe Jess's father was overexcited. Ordinarily, he hated fighting. This time he stepped towards Tom. "It'll take a bigger man than you to do it, Tom Slaney——" he began.

"Please, Joe, please," Mrs. Wright begged.

That was one voice Jess's father always listened to. He swung around and started off. Jess and his mother hurried after him.

CHAPTER SEVEN

THE ABOLITION meeting accomplished one thing; it brought the question of slavery out in the open. Jess discovered that when he went to school the next morning. Sven was waiting for him and told him, "A lot of people are on your father's side now, after the meeting last night."

"Were you there? I didn't see you."

"Sure. Our whole family was there," Sven said.

Other boys greeted Jess with new respect and lined up with him and Sven when Sim and his Snake Mountain crowd swaggered into the school yard. Sim started off with a silly remark. "You and your old man think you're pretty big, don't you? You think you can break any old laws you want to."

Everybody laughed at that. When did the rough, dark people who lived on the mountain start respecting the law? It was a common saying in the valley that they'd steal anything that wasn't nailed down. A girl in Jess's class called out, "Don't pay any attention to him, Jess."

Sim saw that most of the older children were on Jess's side. The bell rang, and Jess joined the line at the boys' door. Sim reached over to tap him on the shoulder. "All the same, you and your old man had better stay close to home. I'm warning you."

"I wonder what Sim's got in mind," Sven fretted. "Maybe his father figures they can get away with doing something to you folks, and the law won't protect you."

"They've been saying things like that ever since my father had Tom Slaney arrested for stealing. We can't start in at this late date worrying about their threats," Jess told Sven.

He didn't mention this to his parents. They had enough on their minds. Besides, he couldn't take it seriously. He figured that Sim's father was so full of bluster and brag, he wouldn't actually dare do anything.

True to his word, Ephraim Woods called a meeting of the Board of Elders, and Mr. Wright was duly notified. The day came. The Wrights ate supper early, so he could get there on time.

Jess's mother tried to send her husband off in a reasonable mood. "Don't quarrel with Mr. Woods if you can help it," she advised. "If we're fair, we have to admit that everybody has a right to his own opinions, the same as we do. Besides, Mr. Woods has a lot of power in Jericho."

"He has no power over me," Mr. Wright growled. "I'm not beholden to him. He doesn't hold any mortgage on our place, and we don't owe him a nickel."

"I wasn't thinking of us. I was thinking of the church."

It still rankled in Mr. Wright's mind that some of the church ladies had been rude to his beloved wife. "What do I care about the church?" he demanded.

"You care a great deal," she told him. "We were married in it and our boys were baptized in it. Maybe there are a few people in it that we don't care for, but that doesn't mean we don't respect it. It's important to us. There are a lot of fine people in it, so let's think of them.

"I'm only asking you to hang onto your temper," she

said. "I'm thinking of the minister and his family. A real dissension inside the church could hurt Mr. Mills. So Joe, please don't get too angry and insult Mr. Woods."

The scowl left her husband's face as he bent down to kiss her. "You're right, as usual," he told her. "I'll do my best, Viney. I won't insult Eph Woods if I can help it."

He was going out the door when he added, "Not unless he insults me or the pastor first!"

The meeting was to be held at the Reverend Mill's home at eight o'clock. Mr. Wright ought to be back by midnight. A long evening of waiting lay ahead. Jess and his mother sat at the kitchen table, the warmest spot in the house. The oil lamp made a cheerful circle on the turkey-red cloth. Jess worked on his arithmetic problems.

His mother was braiding a big rug for the parlor. She had been working on it all winter, and by now it measured six feet across, and was heavy for her to handle. Tonight she was sewing the braids on, using heavy carpet thread. When she had to shift the rug, Jess stopped his studying and lifted it for her.

They didn't talk much. The clock on the fireplace mantel ticked loudly. Each time the stove died down, Jess put new chunks of wood in, and shook down the ashes. It grew late. His mother put away her work and made tea, and after they had had theirs she set the teapot on the back of the stove to keep warm for her husband.

Shortly before midnight they heard the iron rims of the buggy singing along the lane. Jess put on his coat and went to take care of Major. "How did it go, Pa?" he asked.

"Let's wait until we get in the house. Then I can tell you and your mother at the same time."

She had his tea and some warm muffins waiting for him. They both watched his face. He seemed to be in good spirits. His color was high, and he joked with his wife about piling too much sugar in his cup. "Come, Joe, out with it," she commanded. "How did the meeting go?"

"Viney, you would have been proud of me," he said. "I kept my temper."

"That's good," she said, relieved.

"I kept my temper until the meeting was half over. That was about as long as I could manage."

"Oh, Joe," she groaned. "Who was there?"

"Everybody, all twelve members of the Board. None of them looked very happy, and I got a distinct feeling that they hadn't wanted to come. Some went out of their way to be friendly and asked how you and the boys were.

"The meeting began peaceably enough. Maybe Eph Wood's wife had spoken to him, too, for he wasn't as stiff-necked as I expected. He led the meeting, of course, and said he didn't want to make trouble, he just wanted everybody to come to an agreement. As for himself, he thought that slavery was not a question that ought to divide good church people.

"That's when you'd have been proud of me, Viney," Mr. Wright grinned. "I let that pass, bearing in mind what you'd said about each man having a right to his own opinion. For the minister's sake I was willing to keep my mouth shut, hoping the meeting would end with no positive action, only a vague agreement that the church didn't have to make a stand. That wouldn't be binding on the individual members.

"Eph spoiled that. I guess he thought that silence meant consent. I looked around the table and realized that probably each man there except me was indebted to Eph, one way or another. Ed Barrett, for instance, has borrowed money from the bank to keep his store going. Eph's

71

bank holds mortgages on the farms of some of the elders, and he's made personal loans to others.

"Mr. Mills isn't as free as I am, either. Eph Woods is the biggest contributor to his church. It's what Eph puts in the plate on Sunday that makes the difference whether the church is kept up, whether it gets painted, and so forth. There's even a question whether the rest of us could pay the pastor's salary, without Eph's help.

"All this ran through my mind. Then Eph spoke again. 'I can see we're all agreed,' he said. 'I hope we can also agree that a man who breaks the law ought not to serve as an elder of the church.'

"Viney, at that I went cold, and then my hackles started to rise," Mr. Wright said. "The others sat there, kind of stunned. I guess they hadn't expected Eph to try to force me out. I said, 'Obviously, I'm the elder you want to get rid of, Eph. Well, I'm not ashamed to admit that I'll keep on breaking the law, if it's a wicked one like the Fugitive Slave Act.'"

" 'Are you setting yourself up as an authority on the law?' Eph asked, with a real sneer in his voice. 'The government says Negro slaves must be caught where found and returned.'

"Eph went on, but I missed what he was saying, for I was thinking of something else. I recalled that Eph had bought shares in a cotton mill in the eastern part of this state, after he got rich by his father's will. I thought to myself that Eph would lose money if the slaves all left the South, and there wasn't anybody left to raise the cotton for his mill. I thought to myself, Ephraim Woods isn't interested in principles. He's only interested in money.

"I broke into what he was saying. 'Eph,' I said, 'Which are you really worried about, your duty as a churchman or your duty to your pocketbook? You've got friends in the South, and they don't like it, do they, when they lose a two thousand dollar slave? No, they think their Northern friends should get hold of that slave and send him back. Your pocketbook tells you slavery is a good thing, isn't that right? You don't listen to your heart. No, you can't, because your pocketbook is talking too loudly.' "

Jess's father had lost his cheerfulness. His wife caught her breath sharply. He said heavily, "I know what you're going to say, Viney. I went too far. The minister reached over and touched my arm and said, 'Take it easy, Joe,' and I shut up.

"Eph Woods swelled up like a banty rooster and said, 'I want this Board of Elders to vote right now. Whoever is not with me is against me.'

"That sounded like something out of the Bible. I got mad all over again and said, 'How do you dare quote the Good Book, Eph Woods? I'm surprised the words don't turn into toads in your mouth and choke you.' Then I really shut up.

"Eph hates to be called Eph, of course. He thinks that he's at least entitled to Mister, if not to 'My Lord.' He said, 'We'll take the vote now.' He turned to the Reverend Mills and informed him that he had no vote, that only the elected elders could vote. He wanted to make sure that not one man present would be on my side.

"Somebody made the motion, but he only mumbled it. Eph put the question, loud and clear, 'It has been moved and seconded that no confessed law-breaker can serve as a member of the Board of Elders.'

"The minister finally managed to get a word in. He said he wanted to go on record as opposing slavery. Eph advised him to confine his preaching to Sunday. Then he called again for the vote."

Mr. Wright's eyes sparkled as he said, "Viney, I almost

fell out of my chair. I thought that every member of the Board felt he had to vote to dismiss me in order to keep peace between Eph Woods and the church. I thought I was all alone. But Ed Barrett voted against the rest of them!

"Eph demanded to know why. Ed said he thought the minister from Hartford had talked a lot of sense at the abolition meeting. He himself had done a lot of thinking since that night. That was why he had voted as he had.

"The meeting was over, and I got up to go. Then Eph Woods started talking again, and he sounded pretty pleased with himself. He said that if the Board had voted against him, he would have taken himself and his family out of the Jericho church.

"I sang out, 'Why bother to take your family out of the church, Eph? If you and your pocketbook went, you'd succeed in wrecking the church, and you and your pocketbook could be very happy together!'

"Ed Barrett took my arm and pushed me out the door. We walked along the street a ways. I thanked Ed and asked if he hadn't hurt himself. Ed's had a hard time keeping the store going, even with the loan he got from Eph's bank.

"Ed told me frankly he wasn't worried about that bank loan, if that was what I meant. He could manage all right. If he sold a few acres, he could pay off his debt easily. He said he wasn't just proving to Eph that Eph had no hold over him. He was proving it to himself, too.

"I told him that if he really wanted to help fight slavery, he ought to come to see me soon, for we could use every good man we could get, and Ed promised he would."

74

CHAPTER EIGHT

THE WRIGHTS sometimes did their shopping on Saturday. All his life, Jess had looked forward to these trips to town. Like the other farm people, his family took their produce to Barrett's store to exchange it for what they needed, and afterwards stayed for awhile to visit with friends at the store.

On a February Saturday, Jess went to the barn early to gather the eggs. It took him a long time to find them, for the hens ran loose in the barn, laying their eggs where they chose. They seemed to hide them on purpose. Jess climbed to the hayloft and explored along the rafters, looking for nests. One old biddy gave him a hard time, squawking and pecking at him when he lifted her to get the egg from under her.

He brought the eggs to his mother, and she wiped them clean and packed them safely in her market basket. His father brought two crates of apples from the cold cellar and stowed them in the back of the small wagon they used for shopping trips. They set out.

The snow was dazzling white. It was a day of brilliant sunlight, a day that lifted the spirits, made the heart sing. Jess's father was feeling fine. He had sung hymns in a loud voice while he and Jess were doing the chores together. The fact that he had been voted out of the Board of Elders didn't seem to worry him much this morning.

Mrs. Wright, although she tried to be cheerful, couldn't match her husband's mood.

Major trotted smartly, his ears pertly erect, lifting his feet like a yearling. He too acted as though he was glad to be alive on such a day. Jess wondered if Major enjoyed these trips too, wondered if the horses tied to granite posts along Main Street visited together, as their masters did.

Mr. Wright kept glancing at his wife. Finally, he asked, "Viney, what's troubling you?"

"Nothing, Joe."

"Yes, something's the matter."

She confessed, "I guess I dread going to town. I'm getting a little tired of being stared at, as though we were notorious characters."

"Viney, that's my greatest regret, that you should suffer—"

"Don't start that," she ordered, smiling at him. "I believe in what we're doing just as strongly as you and Ben do."

"And Jess," Mr. Wright added.

He drew up before Barrett's General Store and carried in the basket of eggs. Jess wrestled the heavy bushel baskets of McIntosh and Delicious apples out of the back of the wagon and followed.

On any Saturday the store was always crowded, but today everyone seemed to have congregated there. One corner was Jericho's post office, with wooden racks for letters and a window where Mr. Barrett sold postage stamps. It was a popular pastime in Jericho to wait for the mail to be sorted and handed out.

Once again, Jess and his parents received a mixed greeting. Some people shied off as though they were actually

76

afraid to speak to them. Mrs. Barrett was helping her husband wait on customers, and when she saw Lavinia Wright she quickly came around the counter and put her arms around her. They had never been close friends, but Jess guessed she was relieved to greet another woman who was in the same situation. Was Mrs. Barrett beginning to feel the town's disapproval too, now that her husband had declared his feelings about slavery?

Ed Barrett counted out the money for the eggs and apples. Mr. Wright gave the egg money to his wife. They were her hens, so she got the profits. Mrs. Barrett took her to look at the shelf of ginghams and calicoes.

Her husband led Joe Wright out of hearing of the other customers. Jess followed. "Tom Slaney was in this morning," the store keeper said. "He acted bold as brass and ordered a lot of things, although I've refused to let him have any goods until he pays his back bill. He acted as though he'd been drinking. I told him he couldn't take anything until I saw the color of his money. He turned mean, and while he was raging at me made threats against you too, and said he hoped you'd be caught and arrested. Have you been looking for trouble from that quarter?"

"Not really," Mr. Wright said. "Of course, Tom's had it in for me, ever since I had him arrested for stealing some harness. Maybe he thinks that now a lot of people are down on me, and it's a good time for him to get even. But he and his gang are full of brag and bluster, and that's all it is, brag and blow. Jess gets the same thing from his overgrown young'un."

"Just the same, I wonder whether you ought not to leave somebody at your place, when you come to town," Mr. Barrett said. "You didn't happen to meet any of that crowd on the road on your way in?"

"No."

"I haven't changed my mind about wanting to help in your work," Mr. Barrett said earnestly. "You can bring the colored people to my house."

"We'll get together, and I'll explain how the underground operates," Mr. Wright promised.

He seemed uneasy and quickly made his own purchases, and stood over his wife while she decided on the cloth and yarn and ribbons she wanted, then took her arm and led her out.

Ed Barrett followed and handed Jess's father a letter. "I almost forgot. This came yesterday. I didn't want to give it to you in front of people in the store."

Mr. Wright slipped it in his pocket and gave Jess the reins. Mrs. Wright sat between them on the high seat. "Come on, Pa, open the letter," Jess begged. "It's the first time I ever knew of anybody in our family getting one."

"Yes, Joe." Jess's mother added her pleas to his. "Who'd be writing to us?"

Mr. Wright tore it open. "Dear friend," he read, "this is to keep my promise and inform you that we arrived safely. We crossed the border with no trouble and are now living in Montreal. I have found work and can support my family. The Canadian people have been friendly and kind.

"We treasure in our hearts the memory of those who made this new life possible. Here we walk the streets freely and do not fear the law, but only because people like you helped us. The baby is fine and healthy. Martha sends her respectful love to your wife and Jess. We want you to know that we will be grateful as long as we live. When we keep Christmas, it will be a day of memory for the Christmas you gave us. Your friend, John."

Mrs. Wright said happily, "What a lovely surprise!" Then her face clouded. "If we could only know whether Bart lived and got safely across the border."

She took the letter to study it. "None of us could write such a fine letter. John must have gone to good schools in Jamaica when he was a boy. You know, Jess, that's a true love story, such as you might read in a book, his coming to America and meeting Martha, and loving her so much he gave up his freedom to be with her——"

Mr. Wright interrupted. "See if you can get Major to hurry, son."

Jess saw that his father was anxious. He kept Major to a trot until they descended into the valley and turned into their own road.

All was well at home. Nothing was disturbed. When Mrs. Wright had gone to the house, Mr. Wright confided to Jess, "It's just as I thought. Tom Slaney doesn't have the nerve to carry out his threats."

"What were you expecting to find, Father?"

"I don't know. We'll check over the outbuildings, to see if anything's missing, but the place looks all right."

They were sitting down to supper at early dusk, when Sven Swanson and his father dropped in. Mr. Swanson was returning an adz and a plane he had borrowed. "Sit down and share Saturday night beans with us," Mr. Wright hospitably suggested.

"I can't," the neighbor answered. "My wife's waiting supper for us."

"At least you'll have a cup of coffee, then. Jess, put the tools away."

Sven went with Jess to the barn. Jess hung the tools in their proper places over the workbench. They stood in the barn door for a moment, talking.

Sven put up his hand. "Listen, Jess."

"Listen to what?"

"There's something moving under this barn."

"We've got our share of rats and mice—" Jess began.

"Listen!"

The sound Jess heard made his hair stand on end. It was halfway between a sigh and a groan, and it came from under the floor.

Sven looked puzzled, but Jess realized what it was. Someone was hiding in the hole under the barn floor. Now, by the lantern's light, he saw that the trap door was clean. Usually wisps of hay and other litter covered it. Someone had lifted it.

There was no point in denying that something funny was going on. Sven was no fool.

"There's somebody down there," he whispered. "Jess, if you've got the crazy idea I can't be trusted, you're wrong. I'd never tell. Let's get him out."

"How did he come in broad daylight?" Jess wondered aloud. "Somebody left him, but why during the day?" He called out, "It's all right, we're friends," and raised the trap door by its heavy ring. Sven held the lantern over the black hole.

Not one, but two faces stared up, the white eyeballs gleaming, the eyes rolling in fright. A stout Negro woman moaned. The other was a young boy.

"Come out," Jess ordered. "It's safe."

He and Sven reached down to lift the woman out. She seemed like a helpless bundle of rags and slipped out of their hands and sat on the floor. "Can you make it?" Jess asked the boy.

He tried to lift himself, but gave up. "Are you sick?" Jess asked. "What's the matter? Come on, Sven, help me."

They each took a hand, and raised the boy up from the hole. He let out a cry of pain, and Jess said again, "What's the matter?"

Sven said in a low voice, "Look, Jess."

A shawl had slipped from the boy's shoulders. His thin shirt was dark and stiff with blood. Jess lifted it up, and by the lantern's light he and Sven saw that his back was crisscrossed with cuts, and caked with dry blood. It was horribly swollen and discolored, and Jess realized the wounds were infected.

"Get my father," he ordered Sven. "Let yours come too. If we can't trust you Swansons then we can't trust anybody." His voice hardened as he added, "And I guess it's high time everybody up North learned first hand what's going on in the places these people come from."

Sven soon came back with the men. Jess silently held the lantern, so they could see the boy's back. Mr. Swanson let out an exclamation of shock.

"How long have you been on the road, son?" Mr. Wright asked.

"Six days," the boy said. "We came fast."

"Who's the woman?"

"She's my mother. We're trying to find my father. He got away and went North."

"Is that why you were whipped, because your father escaped?"

"Yes, marse."

"How old are you?"

"I'm twelve, marse."

"What's your name? Just give me your first name."

"Amos, and my mother's called Sarah."

"Who brought you this far?"

"A man with a red beard. He left us and went to town

81

to look for you. I'm sorry we made a noise. My mother is very frightened, and I couldn't keep her quiet."

The four helped Amos and Sarah to the house, and Jess's father bolted the kitchen door. Mrs. Wright efficiently went about caring for the newcomers. She wrapped the woman in a quilt, fed her and left her huddled in the chair near the stove. Sven helped Jess lay the boy on the bed in the small room off the kitchen. When Mrs. Wright saw his back, she whispered, "Oh, dear Lord." Then she washed it carefully, spread healing salve on a piece of old, soft sheet, and covered it. Amos lay rigid, clutching the head board, but no cry of pain escaped him.

He gradually relaxed. When Jess took him hot food, he ate a little but fell asleep before it was finished. Mrs. Wright closed the door so he could sleep undisturbed.

They didn't hear a horse, and a knocking on the door startled them, but the knock was the signal of the undergrounders. Mr. Fuller stood there. He came in quickly and looked around the room. "The boys found them in the barn," Mr. Wright reassured him.

"Who are these people?"

"Carl Swanson and his son Sven. They're neighbors who can be trusted."

"Everything's all right then." Mr. Fuller didn't take off his coat and seemed in a hurry to leave.

"How long can we keep them?" Mrs. Wright asked. "Neither of them is fit to travel. The boy especially needs rest and care. Mr. Fuller, you sent that other young man, Bart, on his way much too soon. I know you use your best judgment, and perhaps that time it was necessary. But can't you let these lay over a few days, to give me a chance to heal that young boy's back?"

"What would cause injuries like his?" Mr. Swanson asked. "I never in my life say anything like that." He still looked white and sick. Jess realized that he and his own parents had gotten used to the idea of cruelty. He didn't feel shocked. He only felt angry.

"I can guess what was done," Mr. Fuller said. "The lad wasn't beaten in any fit of rage. He was strung up and whipped by an expert, with a thin whip that was designed to cut. I only got part of his story. He seems like a bright youngster. He was made an example for the others at that plantation where he lived, because his father escaped. He mentioned that other slaves smuggled them out and put them in the care of a Yankee peddler who was heading north. It's a mystery how that peddler hid the two of them for such a distance."

"Can they stay a few days?" Mrs. Wright asked again.

"Maybe two days, not longer. Others are coming. I heard today from a New York man that a party of ten is on its way."

"I'll carry these two to Holden Monday night," Mr. Wright promised.

Mr. Fuller left, and the Swansons were ready to go. Carl Swanson said, "I'm proud that you trusted us, Joe. I wish I could tell you that I was ready to offer to help you in this work."

That seemed like a strange remark. They waited for him to go on. "My wife and I have talked about it," Mr. Swanson explained. "She wants to too, but she's afraid. You see, we're not American citizens. Sven is the only one in our family who was born here. Our girls were born in Sweden. My wife believes we could be sent back if we broke the law."

"Your wife is quite right," Mrs. Wright put in.

"No, I believe she's mistaken," Mr. Swanson said, "and in time I'll persuade her."

"Maybe you'd like to see the place where we hide the fugitives," Mr. Wright said. "Jess, take them up to the attic." He seemed to want his friend to know that he trusted him completely.

Jess took Sven and his father to see the smoke house. "We'll have a place like this soon," Sven said. "We'll win my mother over."

CHAPTER NINE

Mrs. WRIGHT didn't act like herself. She seemed to have lost her courage.

All day Sunday she was pale and distraught as she hovered over Amos. Her gentle touch and her healing salves took the pain out of his cuts.

"She doesn't seem right," Joe Wright said worriedly on Monday morning while he and Jess were working in the barn. "We forget sometimes that she isn't a big strong woman but is really rather frail. She's got more moral courage than any woman I know, but there's a limit to her strength."

Jess had stayed home from school because he was needed. "Jess can make a trip to town for me this morning," Mr. Wright had said at breakfast. "I want to get word to Ed Barrett that I'll need him tomorrow night."

"I don't want Jess to go," Mrs. Wright said.

"Why not, Viney?"

"I've got a feeling."

Her husband tried to tease her out of her mood. "Now that's silly, Viney. Nothing can happen to the boy."

"That's it, he's only a boy," she said stubbornly. "I don't want him to meet those men from up on the mountain."

The reminder of his age annoyed Jess, and he growled, "I can take care of myself."

"No, I'll make the trip," his father decided, putting an end to the argument.

Afternoon came before he was ready to go. Three of the ewes bore lambs that morning, and he and Jess had to build a shelter for them behind the barn. Work kept them away from the house most of the day, but when they went in to get warm or to eat, they noticed that Mrs. Wright seemed more nervous.

She insisted that the two runaways be moved to the smoke house. "Why?" her husband asked. "If you keep the doors locked, nobody can walk in and surprise you."

"I've got a feeling," she said.

"What kind of a feeling?" her husband insisted. "Out with it, Lavinia. What's ailing you?"

"I've just got a sinking feeling that something's going to happen. Ben's on my mind. I wonder if something's wrong with him. I hate to think of night coming. Oh, I don't know, Joe, maybe it's just a woman's silly fancy, but I feel cold in my bones."

"Do as she wants, Jess," Mr. Wright ordered. "Take Amos and his mother up to the attic. I still have to ride to town, and I'd better go now. I'm going to ask Ed to make the trip to Holden tomorrow night. Amos and his mother ought to leave tonight, but another twenty-four hours won't make any great difference, and it'll give you that extra time, Viney, to make sure the youngster is well enough to travel." He began pulling on his boots.

"Do you want me to harness up the buggy?" Jess asked.

"No, I'll ride Major. A fast run will do him good."

The sun was going down in a blaze of orange and pink when they went outside with him. "Why can't you wait till morning?" Mrs. Wright asked.

"I still have to make a living as a farmer," her husband reminded her. "Jess and I need the daylight hours. I won't

86

be gone long. Your fretting is making me nervous, too. Pretty soon you'll give me a real case of the shakes!" He swung up on Major's back, and with a gay wave of his hand set out down the lane.

Jess started for the barn. "Come in the house," his mother commanded.

"Ma, I just want to look at Star. I'm afraid he pulled a tendon in his leg when we were bringing down a load of wood from the hill a couple of days ago."

"That can wait. Please, son, do as I say."

This mood of his mother's was something brand new to Jess. He watched her, concerned, as she drew the kitchen curtains and fixed a tray of food for him to carry up to Sarah and Amos. "I'll have your own supper ready when you come down," she told him.

He was away longer than he had expected, for when he climbed the attic stairs he found that the lamp which lit the stuffy little hiding place had burned up its oil and gone out. The colored woman was crying with fear, and she and Amos huddled on the cot together. Jess realized how alarming it must be to be locked up in the dark and he left his own lamp with them while he fumbled his way through the dark house to bring them a filled one.

He left them eating their supper and started down. His mother's sharp cry rang through the house, "Jess!"

The tone of it startled him so, he almost fell down the back stairs.

"Jess!" She was staring out the kitchen window. Jess saw that a dull glow lit the wide, barn door.

He seized his coat but she tried to hold him back. "I won't let you go out there!"

"Mother, please be sensible," he begged, and got the kitchen door open.

"Listen!" she whispered. Jess heard a horse galloping

away, over the frozen fields. He pushed his mother inside the house and ran across the barnyard.

The drumming of hooves sounded again, but this time it was coming nearer, and to Jess's relief he heard his father's shout in the lane. The two reached the barn together.

A lantern had been flung through the wide door, and had shattered when it hit a wood partition. Burning oil had scattered, and flames were eating a ring on the barn floor and licking up the side of a stall.

"Who did it?" Joe Wright demanded, seizing a heavy burlap bag and beating the fire.

"I don't know. We heard his horse just as you turned off the main road." Jess was flailing away at the flames too.

"Get the horses out. I'll take care of this."

The chickens were squawking, running through the open door. A stone partition separated the cows' stalls from this part of the barn; they were safe unless the roof caught. Star and Leftfoot were neighing and plunging around their box stall.

Mr. Wright seemed to be holding his own against the flames on the floor, and Jess left him. Working frantically, he threw a halter over Leftfoot's neck and led him out and tied him to the rail by the watering trough. He ran back. Star was rearing and striking at the box-stall door. "Steady, boy," Jess tried to soothe him. A quick glance had told him the fire was blazing up the wall, out of his father's reach. The first job, though, was to get Star out before he went crazy with panic. Wary of the murderous hooves, Jess slipped inside the stall and got a halter over his neck and jerked him out.

Once outside the barn, Star quieted and let himself be tied beside his teammate. Jess's heart was pounding so, he felt suffocated as he ran back inside.

His father had climbed the ladder to the hayloft above Jess's head and was pitching hay to clear a space, so the flames couldn't catch the full loft. If the hay really caught, the roof and the whole barn would be doomed.

Jess started up the ladder too, but his father yelled, "No, wet down some burlap!"

It all seemed like a nightmare, and time stood still. Jess's feet felt like lead as he ran to the well clutching a pile of burlap bags. He hauled up a bucket of water and poured it over them. Seconds seemed like hours as he staggered back to the barn with the heavy load.

"Toss them up here!" his father called. Jess began throwing them. Mr. Wright had cleared the hay away, near the burning partition. Now he edged out on a wide beam and began swinging the wet bags at the flames. Jess stared upward, gasping for breath. His father was winning his fight, smothering the greedy, licking tongues of flame.

"Careful, Pa!" Jess was too late. His father, at the end of the beam, reached too far. He let out a cry, threw out his arms and fell.

Sobbing hoarsely with terror and exhaustion, Jess did what had to be done, left his father where he lay on the barn floor, and darted up the ladder. With nothing to cling to, he made his way out on the beam, then straddled it and swung the wet cloths at the fire. Choking, blinded by smoke, he found he was praying. He didn't know whether his father was alive or dead, there below him. He only knew he had to save the barn. The fire was his enemy, his personal enemy. Strength he had never possessed before came to him, and he struck and struck until the flames diminished, flickered out, and died. The partition smoked, and the heat made his head swim, but Jess had won.

He looked down when he reached the ladder, and his heart swelled with relief. By the dull glow of the charring wall he saw that his father had raised himself on one elbow and was watching him.

Jess bent over him. "Pa, are you hurt bad?"

"I reckon my leg is broken."

Utter dark came with the dying of the fire. Jess was desperately wondering what he should do. "Light a lantern," his father ordered.

Jess located the matches and a lantern, and soon its yellow light pushed back the blackness. He set it beside his father. Now he saw that the leg was bent in a strange way. "What are we going to do?" he asked.

"Don't touch the leg. That's a doctor's job. Where's your mother?"

"I don't know. I left her in the house."

"Go and see if she's all right."

Jess found her crouched by a chair in the kitchen, holding her head, looking dazed. "I fainted," she said weakly. "Jess, is the barn gone?"

"No, Ma, we saved it." He helped her to her feet.

"We?"

"Father got home just in time. He's hurt. He fell from the hayloft."

His mother changed before his eyes, hearing that someone needed her care. Jess seemed like the helpless one now, as he leaned against the wall, trying to draw air into his lungs and still his pounding heart.

She seized a wool comforter from the bed in the next room and ran outside. When Jess reached the barn she was bending over her husband, covering him against the cold. All her thought was of him as she ordered, "Ride to town for Dr. Gray, Jess, and tell him to come at once."

"Mother, couldn't we straighten Father's leg, so he'll be more comfortable?" The sight of the leg bent at an unnatural angle made Jess feel sick in his stomach.

"No, we'd do more harm than good." She knelt on the floor, cradling her husband's head in her arms.

Joe Wright's voice was weak but steady. "Just a minute, son. I was hurrying home to tell you that there's a Federal marshal in town who's tracked Amos and Sarah this far. Sheriff Hodgkins told me. He's changed his tune, and says he doesn't want us to be caught harboring them and says somebody else in town is likely to tell where they're hiding. Bring Ed Barrett back with you. He'll have to take the two to Holden tonight. Get back here as soon as you can."

Jess had a moment of panic when he discovered that Major was missing. His father hadn't tied him when he rushed to the burning barn. Jess whistled, and obediently the faithful old horse trotted out of the shadows. Jess caught the reins and swung himself up.

It wasn't until he was racing along the Pumpkin Hollow road that he discovered he was soaked to the skin. While he was wetting down the burlap to fight the fire, he had poured water over himself. Now the whistling wind froze his coat and his pants stiff. He felt as though he was encased in armor.

He came down the hill and crossed the wooden bridge. The town looked peaceful; lamps glowed behind windows along Main Street. He slowed to a walk to avoid calling attention to himself and turned in Dr. Gray's yard.

It seemed like hours before the doctor's wife answered his pounding at the back door. "Why, Jess Wright," she began, startled by his appearance.

The doctor came up behind her. He didn't waste words. "Who's sick?"

"Pa fell from the hayloft and broke his leg. Can you come now?"

"As quick as I can for a fat man," the doctor said. "Mary, get my bag, please."

"It's right in the hall," she said.

"Bring my muffler and my fur hat."

He wanted to get his wife out of the way. When they were alone, he asked, "Jess, are there any fugitive slaves at your farm tonight?"

What could Jess say? He loved the doctor, as everyone in Jericho did, but could he trust him?

"I see you won't answer," Dr. Gray said. "Your father has some enemies who would like to see him caught. Did you know that?"

"Yes," Jess said bitterly. "One tried to burn our barn tonight. Please, Dr. Gray, let's get going."

Mrs. Gray had come back and was winding a long muffler around her husband's neck. "You're not leaving here until my wife dries your clothes and fixes you some hot food," the doctor told Jess. "You'll get pneumonia if you don't thaw out, and I'll have two patients at the Wright place."

Jess protested, but it did no good. The doctor left.

He swallowed the hot soup Mrs. Gray set before him, but when she insisted that he take off his frozen clothes so that she could dry them, Jess refused. "Couldn't you just loan me some of the doctor's?" he pleaded. "I've got to get right home, ma'am."

"They're three times too big for you," she pointed out. Then she sensed that Jess was just about ready to break down and howl, from worry and frustration. She found some dry pants and a warm jacket that had belonged to her grown son. Jess quickly dressed and left.

The streets were empty, but Barrett's General Store was lit up. Jess slid off Major and peered in the front window. A dozen townsmen stood about. Ed Barrett was behind the counter. A stranger was warming himself by the stove.

Jess couldn't hear what was being said, but he knew that the store was a hornets' nest of danger to him right then. There was no way to give Mr. Barrett his father's message.

He rode Major at a slow walk out of town. Once across the bridge he dug his heels into the horse's belly, and Major responded with a burst of speed.

What time was it? Jess wondered. It must be getting on towards midnight. Since dusk, this night had been stretching itself out endlessly.

Somehow, before morning, the two Negroes must be gotten away from Jericho. Jess was now beginning to realize that this was completely up to him.

There was no moon, but the stars gave some light. Jess was out in open country and riding hard when he glimpsed a buggy ahead. Who was out so late? It couldn't be the doctor. He must have reached the Wright farm long before now.

For a mile, Jess dawdled along behind. He longed to be home, to find out how his father was, to get on with the night's work that lay ahead. Finally, he took a chance and came up behind the buggy. Curtains hid the driver, but the buggy looked familiar. Jess drew up alongside.

A face peered out, and Jess shouted with relief. It was the minister.

"Whoa!" The Reverend Mills pulled up his horse. "Jess Wright! What's the matter?"

All Jess wanted to do was to share his troubles, the whole load of them, with someone. The words tumbled out. "Mr. Mills, I'm in a peck of trouble. Somebody tried to burn our barn, and Pa fell and broke his leg. The doctor's there now. We've got two people hid in the attic. The federal marshal is in town. Any minute he'll be on the road, riding this way. Mr. Mills, what'll I do? I've got to get those people away from the farm and headed north!" He was shaking violently with the cold, and his teeth chattered like castanets.

The minister didn't cluck or fuss or hesitate. "Get down off that horse, tie him behind, and get in here under my robe," he ordered. "If you take sick you'll be no help, and you and I have our work cut out for us."

With unutterable relief Jess realized that luck had turned his way. "You mean you'll help me get the fugitives on the next station, Mr. Mills?"

"Why do you think I'm on the road tonight?" the minister asked. "I was on my way to warn your father."

CHAPTER TEN

THEY ENTERED the barn as the doctor was finishing splinting Mr. Wright's leg, tying it between two boards. "What are you doing here, Reverend?" he asked, astonished.

"I just happened to be on the road and met Jess."

"Don't tell me you were out making pastoral calls on a night like this!"

"I came just in time, didn't I?" the minister said, with a chuckle. "You need me to help get Joe into the house."

Following the doctor's directions, Jess unhinged a door, and they put the injured man on it. Mr. Wright couldn't keep from groaning as they carried him to the house and laid him on the bed in the room off the kitchen. His face was as white as the pillow case.

Dr. Gray gave Mrs. Wright some pills to help his pain, promised to come the next morning, and left. It was a relief to all to see him go.

Mrs. Wright raised her husband's head to give him the pills, but he refused them. "I need a clear head," he said. "Reverend, I'm sorry you're mixed up in this, but if you've come to help you're a lifesaver. I couldn't have picked a worse night to get hurt."

"I tried to see Mr. Barrett," Jess told his father. "The federal agent was at his store, along with a lot of other men, and I didn't dare go in."

"That's why I came to warn you," the minister said. "I knew that he was in town and was afraid he'd try to take the Negroes before morning. Jess and I will have to get them away. Tell us what to do."

Mr. Wright tried to sit up, but pain caught him and he fell back. "Let's leave him alone," the minister suggested. "We'll have to take care of this ourselves."

Despite his pain, Jess's father was alert. "No," he said, "I'll tell you what to do, Jess. But first, let's get one thing straight. The minister will have no part in transporting Sarah and Amos. I can't take that on my conscience, that I let him."

"Why not?" the minister demanded hotly. "The Reverend Sykes does."

"The Reverend Sykes has no wife or children. You do, sir. Now, Jess, listen closely. You'll carry Amos and his mother to Holden, and there you'll look for Mr. Jeffers' house. You met him at Christmas time when he came to fetch John and Martha. He lives on South Street. You can't miss his house; it's a big gray one with a cupola on the roof. Go to the back door. You know the signal, Jess, two loud knocks, three soft. Keep knocking until you rouse either Mr. Jeffers or his hired man, who helps in the underground. Have you got that straight?"

"Yes," Jess said. "Now take the pills, Pa, and get some rest. I'll manage."

Almost as soon as he closed his eyes, Mr. Wright fell heavily asleep.

Jess brought Amos and Sarah down, while his mother prepared a package of food for them. The Reverend Mills was obviously dismayed by their appearance. Sarah still wore her rags, with Mrs. Wright's warmest shawl wrapped around her. She cried steadily, the tears rolling

98

down her wide face. Thin, wiry Amos was lost inside a heavy shirt of Ben's. He clutched the tattered blanket he had brought with him.

"We can't send them away in those clothes," the minister protested.

This sounded like a criticism of his parents' care of the fugitives, and Jess couldn't stand that. "Mr. Mills, we've given away all the clothes we can spare. We're starting on Ben's now. When he comes home from prison he won't have an extra shirt. When this boy came, the one he wore was in shreds and caked with blood. His back was infected. Show him, Amos."

The boy did as Jess ordered. Distressed, Mr. Mills exclaimed, "Jess, Mrs. Wright, forgive me. I didn't understand." He took off his own cape and put it around Amos.

"Now how do you think you're going to face the cold, yourself?" Mrs. Wright asked.

"Can you lend me a blanket? Jess can bring it back."

They were ready. Mrs. Wright clung to Jess. "Son, I hate to see you go!"

"You've got your hands full taking care of Father," Jess told her, patting her on the back. "I'll make out all right. Don't worry. Lock this door as soon as we're gone. If the marshal comes you can let him search the house. I covered over the door to the smoke house."

She held the lamp at the kitchen window to guide them, as Jess and the minister helped the runaways into the buggy and covered them with the heavy robe after they crawled over behind the seat. The minister had insisted that Jess borrow his own buggy, as it was tight and warm. Jess was to drop him off in town. He put his foot on the step to follow. "Listen," Jess said.

They heard a horse, far off but coming fast along the

bottom lands. The circle of hills made the sound reverberate. To Jess's experienced ears it began to sound like two horses.

Frantically, he tried to figure out what to do. Should he take the runaways back into the house? Should he hide them in the hole under the barn? Or should he try to brazen the situation out?

Actually, there wasn't time to make any move. The horses tore up the lane. Jess made out the heavy figure of Jericho's sheriff. The other man had to be the government marshal.

The minister said, "I'll take these people to my house, Jess. Come as soon as you can."

"Mr. Mills, I can't let you try it. My father wouldn't like that—" Jess began.

There was no time to argue. The riders dismounted. Sheriff Hodgkins said to his companion, "Let me handle this. I know these people—" He stopped, for he had recognized the buggy. He sounded surprised, but respectful. "What are you doing out at this time of night, Reverend?"

"I'm paying a pastoral call," Mr. Mills said.

The marshal snorted. The sheriff turned on him angrily. "I told you I'd handle this, if you insisted on coming. I told you it was probably a wild goose chase and we wouldn't find anything. Be careful how you speak, because in this town we show proper respect for our minister."

"It seems like a peculiar hour to be paying pastoral calls," the other man remarked.

The minister coldly addressed Jericho's sheriff. "Perhaps you didn't know that Mr. Wright fell from his hay loft and broke his leg," he said. "Perhaps you didn't know that someone tried to burn his barn. I dare say you've

100

been too busy slave-catching tonight, Mr. Hodgkins, to find time to look after your own duties."

"Reverend, that's not fair," the sheriff protested. "I'm no slave catcher!"

"What are you doing here, then?"

"I only came with this federal man because the law says I have to."

"We'll argue that some other time." Mr. Mills took up the reins.

"Wait," the federal agent ordered.

"What is your name, sir?" the minister demanded.

"Burns. Reverend, I hope you're not mixed up with the undergrounders."

"I thank you for your concern, sir."

"I believe that as a matter of form you should step down and let us search your buggy. That will clear you, in case you're ever suspected."

"You'll search my buggy for what?"

"For contraband, for other people's property."

"You consider human beings as property," the minister said quietly.

"Yes, slaves are property, certainly."

"Slaves are people and entitled to protection under God. Take your hand off my horse's head, sir, or you'll feel the cut of my whip!"

"Now, Reverend," the sheriff protested.

For answer, the minister drew back his thin buggy whip and flicked it near the federal agent's head. He jumped back, cursing. The minister jerked the reins and his horse obeyed, and the buggy went jolting down the lane.

The three watched him go. Jess was doing some fast thinking. If he himself behaved suspiciously, maybe he could take this agent's mind off the minister. He sidled towards the house.

Mr. Burns was with him in two strides. "You, whatever your name is, don't you try to fool with me. I've got a search warrant. We'll find those Negroes if they're here."

Jess knocked at the door, calling, "Ma, let us in." His mother opened it and let out a cry at sight of the men.

"Sorry to disturb you, ma'am," Mr. Burns said. "It's my duty to search this house. I have a warrant."

Anger got the better of her fear. "Then you can start here in my kitchen and in the bedroom," she said. "You'll find only a badly injured man. But look under his bed, if you want to."

"There's no need for that, Lavinia," Sheriff Hodgkins looked embarrassed and miserable. "I'm sorry Joe got hurt. I'll try to catch the person who fired your barn. Was it one of the mountain gang?"

The federal man wasn't interested in any local barn-burning. "Show us the rest of the house, sonny," he ordered.

Jess led the two all over the house, taking a lot of time doing it. The more time they wasted here, the more time the minister had for hiding Sarah and Amos. When they reached the cellar he pretended he was afraid to let them go down. "The stairs are steep. You'll fall. There's nothing down there," he insisted.

Mr. Burns brushed him aside and took the kitchen lamp to light his way. The others stayed upstairs. They heard him pushing heavy barrels around, grunting and muttering. When he came up he was dirty and sweating and said curtly to the sheriff, "We'll come back by daylight. We'll find where they hide their runaways."

Jess couldn't help grinning. "You haven't looked in the attic yet."

"You watch yourself, sonny!" The marshal stalked out of the house. He and the sheriff rode away.

Mrs. Wright was sitting beside her husband, who continued to sleep deeply. When she saw that Jess was getting ready to leave she clutched him. "Jess, it's two o'clock in the morning. How can I let you go alone at such an hour?"

"We've got no choice, Ma," Jess pointed out. "I'll try to get back by daylight."

"Oh, if only Ben was here!"

It was wrong, but Jess was beginning to feel meanly thankful that Ben was safely locked up in jail. The whole show was Jess's. Having the federal agent call him "sonny" only made Jess more determined. If he succeeded tonight, nobody would ever treat him as a stupid young boy again.

His mother tucked in his scarf. "Oh Jess, I never felt so helpless in my life. You're my baby!"

He bent and kissed her. "No, mother," he said, "I'm not your baby. Just look after Pa. Don't worry about me."

In utter darkness he harnessed Major to the small wagon, and drove down the lane. He was well aware how far the clatter of a trotting horse carried and held Major down to a slow pace. Loneliness came over him like a wave. The whole world slept. Only he was awake and abroad in the night.

When he reached the main road, he suddenly made up his mind. If Sven wanted to help, tonight was the night Sven should get his chance.

Easing Major along, he turned in at the Swansons' lane.

No lights flickered in the windows. Sven's room was on the north side, over the kitchen lean-to. Jess made a snowball and tossed it at the window.

It slid up, and Sven peered out. "Come on," Jess ordered in a hoarse whisper. "Hurry!"

Sven asked no questions. A minute later the window slid all the way up, and Sven, fully dressed, put his leg over the sill. He slid down the roof and dropped beside Jess. "Do you want to tell your folks you're going with me?" Jess asked.

"No. If I wake them up, they'll argue. My father's just about talked my mother into joining the underground, but they still wouldn't want me to go," Sven explained. He scrambled up to the wagon seat.

It wasn't until they had started that he said, "Is that right, that we're going on underground business? Where are we going?"

"To Holden."

Sven turned to look in the back of the wagon. "Where are the passengers?"

"They're at the minister's, I hope." While they jogged along, Jess told him everything that had happened.

Jess again had the queer feeling that time was standing still. Was it only a few hours ago that he and his father had fought the fire? It seemed as though weeks had passed since then.

He was so tired and so tense, every shadow made him nervous. He expected the marshal, Burns, to jump out from behind every bush.

He slowed Major to a crawl as they crossed the bridge, to prevent the horse's feet from clattering on the wooden planks. They passed the doctor's house, the store, the town hall. Every building was dark. They came to the church. The parsonage stood next to it, and all its windows were blank too.

Jess drove around in back and sat for a moment. He had no idea what to do. Maybe Jericho was sleeping, but he had the feeling that if he made the slightest noise he would stir up a terrible row. Maybe the windows of the houses along Main Street were dark, but they were like eyes, watching and waiting for him to make a move.

"Jess!"

Jess and Sven jumped down from the wagon. Where did the whisper come from?

"Jess Wright!" The minister was calling them from the side door of the church.

"They're inside, safe," Mr. Mills whispered, as the boys joined him.

A faint light shone through the high windows and vaguely lit the altar. Jess and Sven snatched off their wool caps. They heard a stir at the back of the church and saw two shapeless figures there. Sarah's arms were around her son.

"Just a minute before you take them," the minister said. He led Sarah and Amos up the aisle and they knelt at the altar. Mr. Mills prayed for their safety, spreading his arms over them as though sheltering them.

"Thank you, marse," Sarah said softly, as she got to her feet.

"Sarah, you and your son will soon be in Canada," the minister told her, "where you'll never have to call any man 'master' again. May God watch over you."

They went out into the cold night. He asked, "Aren't you going to take my buggy? It's warmer."

"No," Jess said. "That federal marshal knows it by sight now. I forgot to fill this wagon with hay. Could you let us have some?"

He backed the wagon into the minister's barn and forked down enough to cover the floor behind the seat. Sarah and Amos lay down on it. The mother seemed to have found new courage and, forgetting her own terror, was thinking only of her boy. She put her arms around him, Jess tucked a blanket over them both, then covered them with more hay.

Mr. Mills had been silent. Now he burst out, "I cannot let you go! Tell me where to take them, Jess. This kind of risk is for grown men, not for boys!"

"Sir, we'll be all right," Jess said earnestly. "It's my job. My father trusted me with it."

"How old are you, Sven?"

"Fifteen, sir."

"Fifteen, and Jess is fourteen," the minister mused. "Well, if you succeed and get these poor souls to safety, no one who knows about it will ever think of you as less than men. God go with you."

CHAPTER ELEVEN

ALL RIGHT, Major," Jess said softly.

The church clock boomed just as they rumbled into Main Street, and he almost jumped out of his skin. One, two, three. The booms were loud enough to wake the dead.

How cold was it? The thermometer had read ten above earlier in the evening, but that was a long time ago. In this deep hour of the night the cold always intensified. Sven shivered, and Jess ordered, "Move over," and wrapped the buffalo robe tightly around them both. The cold still seeped in, and Sven continued to shiver. Jess could have asked, "What's the matter, are you scared?"

He didn't. If Sven was scared, that was Sven's own business. He certainly had a right to be. Sven had wanted to come, and he was here, and so far he had made no complaints, and that was all Jess had to know. He himself held the comforting thought that probably after they got through this night, he and Sven would be the closest friends as long as they lived.

For that matter, he himself was scared enough for two. He tried to fix his mind on cheerful thoughts. He remembered that Ben would soon be coming home, and his lighthearted laughter would cheer up the Wright house. February would soon be over. In March, the year would turn the corner towards spring. The river would unfreeze, the ice that locked the fields would melt, and brown meadows would start turning green.

How he wished he had greased the wagon wheels. His father had told him to, days ago, but so much had happened it had slipped Jess's mind. Now they were singing out of tune in loud, jarring shrieks and groans, as the wagon climbed Town Hill.

They started down the other side, leaving Jericho behind. Leaving danger behind?

Jess's imagination was working overtime. He could imagine people lying in bed listening to the creaks of the wagon and Major's slow clop-clop and thinking, Somebody's transporting slaves tonight. Mr. Ephraim Woods, his father's enemy, would love to see another member of the Wright family caught. The federal marshal, who only cared about the fee he would earn by catching Sarah and Amos, did he hear? And how about Sheriff Hodgkins, who couldn't make up his mind which side he was on? Jess could imagine them mounting horses, getting ready to pursue. He kept glancing nervously back along the road.

"Can't we go faster?" Sven whispered.

"Pretty soon, when we get to a level stretch. But the faster we go the more noise we'll make. The next time my father tells me to grease this wagon, believe me I won't let any grass grow under my feet!"

Sven giggled nervously.

They reached the flat lands north of Jericho, and Jess ordered, "Giddap, Major." Obligingly, the horse quickened his pace, but the dry axles groaned louder than ever. Jess pulled Major back to a walk.

Sven's voice sounded like a shout. "I'm going back and see how Amos and Sarah are making out."

"Shut up!" Jess snapped.

He scared himself. The truth was, he suddenly realized, he was on the ragged edge of panic. His mind told him the danger was behind them, and no one was pursuing. But his nerves were leaping like live things under his skin. Every dark shadow could hide a man with a loaded gun. Every bush seemed ready to move and jump into the road.

He said, "I'm sorry, I didn't mean to snap your head off. Yes, go back and look, will you?"

Sven scrambled over the seat and parted the hay. "Are you folks all right?"

Sarah answered. "Yes, marse, we's all right. How far we got to go?"

"Not far," Sven told her. "Do you want anything to eat, Amos?"

"No, thanks," the boy said.

"If you do, you let us know." Sven climbed up beside Jess and pulled his share of the buffalo robe around him. They jogged on.

As for Jess, he was still ashamed of himself for snapping at his friend. He ought to be proud and happy. For months, even before Ben was arrested, he had prayed for a chance like this. It wasn't easy to be the youngest in the family and to have to untie yourself from your mother's apron strings. Every time slaves had come, to be hidden and taken on to the next station, he had hoped for a chance to be the hero, the one to take the danger. He hadn't exactly wished Ben would be arrested or hoped his father would break a leg. But still, in the back of his mind he had wanted something like this to happen.

Hero! he thought now. Some hero. He felt more like a sniveling coward. He only longed for a hole to hide in. He'd hoped his father would trust him. Now he wished

111

his father had refused. He'd wanted to prove he was a man. Now he thought, who wants to be a man?

He saw that Sven was glancing at him curiously and realized he was trembling. With fear? Yes, Jess admitted to himself, he was terrified.

By an act of will he controlled his shaking, and explained, "It's awfully cold."

Sarah's voice, not a foot away from his ear, startled him so he almost fell off the high seat. "Marse, where's the star?"

"What does she mean?" Sven asked.

"That North Star," Sarah said.

"These people think they've got a special star that leads them up to Canada," Jess explained. He studied the heavens, and located the Big Dipper, due north above the low, dark hills. All the stars shone with special brightness, burning in the cold, clear air. "Look, Sarah, where I'm pointing. Count the ones in the handle of the Big Dipper, and you'll see the bowl. Take a line along the outer edge of the bowl, and you'll see it. That's your star."

"I don't see it, but that's my star," Sarah repeated contentedly.

"Now get back under the hay and cover yourself up, and keep warm," Jess ordered.

The talking had calmed him. He thought, What does it matter how scared I am? The important thing is to get Amos and Sarah out of reach of the slave catchers. What's the worst that can happen to Sven and me? We could be arrested and sent to jail, that's all. Of course Ma wouldn't like that. But if I go to jail, that'll prove I'm as good as Ben.

The road started climbing. They had been traveling through empty country, but now they passed a farm.

112

"Look, there's a light in that barn," Sven whispered. "Somebody's doing his milking. It must be almost morning."

A rooster crowed, another answered from the next farm, then another. Far away, dogs began to bark. In the east, the blue-black sky was turning gray. "Can't you get this old horse to pick up his feet and go a little faster?" Sven asked.

"Listen, you're not half as nervous as I am." Jess laughed, but it came out like a croak.

"Do you mean to say you're scared?"

"Boy, am I! I'm just about ready to jump out of my skin."

There, he had said it. Jess suddenly felt about a thousand times better.

They reached the crest of a hill, and there below lay Holden, the frosted roofs gleaming, the road shining like a narrow silver ribbon. The descent was steep, and when Jess applied the brake to the iron wheel, it shrieked like a banshee.

He had been to Holden only a few times, when he went with his parents to visit Ben. Houses and fences were clearly visible as he entered Main Street. Now lamps flickered behind many of the windows. He drove slowly along, looking for a big gray house with a cupola, and found it.

"We're here," he said. "You two back there, keep under the hay. No matter what happens, stay under the hay."

Sarah whispered loudly, "Marse?"

"What, Sarah?" Jess asked.

"Thank you, young marse, for bringing us."

"That's all right," he said. "Now don't talk any more."

He turned into the driveway. He dreaded leaving the wagon while he got down to inquire. An enormous barn

113

loomed behind the house, and he almost shouted with relief. Its wide door was open.

A man emerged from the next house, and watched as Jess boldly drove Major into the barn and stopped. He didn't glance at the man. He and Sven started for the house.

A voice behind them demanded, "Who be you?"

They whirled. A tall farmer with a rough beard had emerged from the barn and towered over them.

"Who are you?" Jess asked.

"I'm Mr. Sam Jeffers' hired man."

"That's all right, then," Jess said loudly. "We brought the load of hay that Mr. Jeffers ordered."

The hired man winked and jerked his head at the watching neighbor. Then he growled, "You took your time about it. You're a day late. Go in the house and get your pay. I'll unload your wagon."

The boys obeyed. Jess put his hand on the back door and it opened before he could push.

Old Mr. Jeffers pulled him and Sven inside. The kitchen was warm and fragrant with the smell of good cooking, and Jess was overcome with faintness. He sat down on the nearest chair.

Blue eyes bored into his. "Explain yourself, boy."

"You came to our house once, Mr. Jeffers. I'm Jess Wright, Joe Wright's son. I've brought some passengers. Look, Mr. Jeffers, I brought you trouble, too. We wanted to get here while it was still dark, but we didn't make it. Your next door neighbor saw us drive in. Your hired man's out in the barn with the two passengers."

"Maybe you brought me trouble, sonny, but no more than I can handle. I can deal with nosy neighbors," Mr. Jeffers said. He poured coffee and pushed a plate of doughnuts towards Jess and Sven.

114

"Where are you going to hide them?" Jess asked.

"That's my business, not yours, sonny. I wouldn't ask you where you hide them at your house, would I? Come to think of it, why did Joe Wright send a couple of young un's to do a man's work?"

"My father broke his leg last night. He's hurt real bad. There's a federal marshal in Jericho named Burns. He came to our house last night. He's probably headed this way——"

"You boys did fine," Mr. Jeffers broke in, "but now if you've warmed yourselves, take the rest of the doughnuts and go. I hate to seem inhospitable, but I want to get rid of you. If there are any slave catchers in the area, I can handle them. I want you to get home just as fast as you can, and when you get there, tell Joe Wright I said you did just fine."

Before the boys quite realized how it happened, the door shut in their faces. With their pockets full of doughnuts, they climbed up on the wagon seat. The passengers and the load of hay had disappeared.

Jess picked up the reins and clucked to Major. The hired man watched, grinning broadly. Jess drove out.

"That old man was a funny character," Sven remarked.

"I guess he had his own reasons for acting so snappy," Jess said.

They were passing the jail. He was hoping against hope that one of the barred windows facing the street was Ben's, that Ben would happen to be looking out. He would see his young brother driving bold as brass down Holden's main street, and he would guess what errand had brought him.

Sven must have read Jess's mind. "When is your brother's time up?" he asked.

"In a couple of weeks."

That thought gave Jess such a joyful jolt, all the fears of the night vanished. He couldn't help it, he let out a sudden shout. "Yahoo! Ben, Ben Wright! Here I am. It's me, Jess!"

There! If Ben was within earshot, he had heard that yell!

Sven was grinning like a Cheshire cat. Giddy with relief, Jess started pummeling him. "We made it!" he cried. "Everything's all right!"

Light-hearted and feeling silly, they started to sing. They roared every song they knew to the astonished countryside. Jess slapped the reins on Major's back. "Giddap, you old mule!" Major was feeling brisk himself and glad that at last his nose was pointed homeward. He smartly picked up his heels. And so they careened along the road, yelling and singing, back to Jericho.

Major tired first. Fun was fun, but he didn't mean to be put upon. He slowed down, and when Jess tried to make him gallop he turned his head and shook his harness and glared.

They started down the last long hill into town. Who cared now if the brake shrieked? The church clock struck nine as they turned into Main Street. Women, bundled up against the cold, were crossing the Green to do their shopping. Mr. Ephraim Woods was mincing along on his way to his bank. In front of Barrett's store men were idly lounging.

What got into Jess he never knew, afterward. He just felt too gloriously happy to contain himself. He spied the federal marshal, Burns, emerging from the Jericho Hotel. He saw Sheriff Hodgkins in the group of townspeople in front of Barrett's store. Jess drew Major up short. "Good morning, sheriff!" he sang out.

Mr. Hodgkins stared. "How's business this morning?" Jess called.

Now everyone was staring. Sven grabbed Jess's sleeve, because he was standing up in the wagon. "Shut up!" he hissed.

Jess shook him off. "Did you catch any slaves this morning, Mr. Hodgkins?" Jess called. "How's the slave catching business? Did you and your pal Burns have any luck?"

Hearing the commotion, Ed Barrett emerged from his store. He stood on the porch, grinning over the crowd.

The sheriff was a big man, but he managed to hustle over to the wagon. "What ails you, Jess Wright?"

"I just asked you a civil question," Jess said. "Did you catch those runaways you were looking for?"

The sheriff was blustering, but the voice of the federal agent was icy cold. "Take those boys for questioning."

The tone of that voice froze Jess, and his high spirits evaporated. He'd made a fool of himself. Now he was in trouble that he himself had created. Burns repeated, "Take them to the jail. I want to ask some questions."

Sheriff Hodgkins was at Major's head, his hand on the strap. Now he turned, putting his solid bulk between the federal marshal and the boys. "I'm not going to do any such thing," he said. "They've done no harm. They've committed no crime. What's the matter with a couple of boys doing a little yelling if they feel like it? They ought to be in school, though. If I'm going to arrest them, it'll be for truancy." He said over his shoulder urgently, "Jess, get going. Get out of town."

"Yes, sir." Jess picked up the reins. The men in the street moved aside to let the wagon through.

"Stop!" Burns called after them.

Sheriff Hodgkins spoke loud enough for all to hear, as

117

the wagon lurched away. "I'm the law in this town, don't forget that, Mr. Burns. I don't arrest crazy-headed boys just for yelling. Come on, folks, clear the street. The excitement's over."

Sven and Jess didn't exchange a word, as they crossed the town bridge. Major needed no urging now; he was heading towards home and his comfortable stall and his breakfast. "You don't have to tell me," Jess mumbled. "That was a fool thing to do."

"Maybe so," Sven agreed, burrowing under the buffalo robe to get warm. "Maybe so, but I'm not sorry. That federal marshal looked mad enough to burst!"

They reached Jess's lane first. "Do you want me to take you straight home?" he asked.

"No, let's go see how your father is. If my father's mad already, being a few minutes later isn't going to make him any madder."

They swung into the barnyard. The Swansons' mare was tied at the rail, and Sven's father opened the kitchen door. "So you're back," he said.

"Yes, sir," Sven answered respectfully.

"It didn't occur to you to wake me up and tell me what you were up to before you sneaked off in the night?"

"Yes, sir, it occurred to me," Sven admitted, "but it just didn't seem like a very good idea."

His father's face cleared, and his hearty laugh rang out.

That brought Mrs. Wright to the door. Her face lit up, but she only said too, "So you're back, Jess."

"Yes, ma'am."

"Is that Jess?" Mr. Wright's voice sounded strong.

"Go in to your father," Mrs. Wright ordered.

Jess and Sven stood at the foot of the bed. For a long moment, Mr. Wright stared at them. He looked fine, this morning; the ruddy color was back in his face. "You made it," he said.

"Yes, Pa."

"You had no trouble?"

"No," Jess said steadily, "none I didn't make for myself. We happened to meet the sheriff and that federal man in town, on our way home. I guess I made a fool of myself, trying to make them look stupid. I'm sorry."

"Never mind about that. You found Mr. Jeffers in Holden and turned the passengers over to him personally?"

"His hired man took charge of them."

His father sank back on his pillows. "Good," he said. "Two more are safely on their way to Canada. You boys did a good night's work."

Mrs. Wright soon had bacon and eggs frying. Sven tackled his plate, and Jess was about to when he remembered and started up. "I forgot all about the milking!"

"Mr. Swanson did your chores," his mother told him. "Sit down and eat. Then Sven will go home and you'll go to bed."

Sven finished, and when he stood up to go he staggered with tiredness. The boys said goodbye casually, as though this was just like any ordinary day. Jess watched his friend riding the mare, while his father walked alongside across the fields to their house.

The red tablecloth looked so inviting, Jess put his head down beside his unfinished breakfast to rest.

The next thing he knew, his mother was shaking him. "Come, son, come with me. You're going to bed."

She put her arms around him to help him up the stairs. Jess protested, "Ma, I can make it. I don't need any babying. I'm a big boy now!"

119

She led him to his room and turned down the bed covers. "I know," she said. "You're right. You're a big boy now."

There was pride in her face, but there was sadness there, too. "You'll just have to be patient with me, Jess," she said softly. "It'll take me a little time to get used to the idea that both my boys are men."